MISS TIBBLES KNEW
SHE OUGHT TO OBJECT

She even, she noted with a detached sense of horror, clutched his coat with her fingers.

Gently he detached those fingers and kissed them, one by one. And still she did not object. He tilted up her chin, and before she knew what he meant to do, he bent his head close to hers and gently kissed her.

At least it was meant to be a gentle kiss. Marian would have staked her life on that. But it didn't remain a gentle kiss. She heard a muffled curse, though she could not have said whether it came from her throat or his, and then the kiss deepened.

Her fingers were once again clutching the lapels of his coat. And her body arched itself against him as a moan unmistakably escaped her own lips.

This was not what she planned. This was not, her head told her, what she wanted. But it was what she did. And when the tip of his tongue hesitantly touched her lips, she parted them willingly. . . .

Miss Tibbles' Folly

by

April Kihlstrom

A SIGNET BOOK

SIGNET
Published by the Penguin Group
Penguin Putnam Inc., 375 Hudson Street,
New York, New York 10014, U.S.A.
Penguin Books Ltd, 27 Wrights Lane,
London W8 5TZ, England
Penguin Books Australia Ltd, Ringwood,
Victoria, Australia
Penguin Books Canada Ltd, 10 Alcorn Avenue,
Toronto, Ontario, Canada M4V 3B2
Penguin Books (N.Z.) Ltd, 182–190 Wairau Road,
Auckland 10, New Zealand

Penguin Books Ltd, Registered Offices:
Harmondsworth, Middlesex, England

First published by Signet, an imprint of Dutton NAL,
a member of Penguin Putnam Inc.

First Printing, September, 1998
10 9 8 7 6 5 4 3 2 1

Prologue

It wasn't that Miss Tibbles wished to take advantage of Lord and Lady Westcott. It was simply that all five daughters were wed and no one quite knew what to do with her, least of all Miss Tibbles herself.

She ought to be searching for another position. She knew it as well as they did. But after some eighteen years of being a governess, always to the most challenging of girls, rarely staying in one place more than the year or two required to draw the girl into proper behavior and find her a husband, Miss Tibbles was tired. She had become accustomed, moreover, to the Westcott household. It was the longest she had ever stayed in one place as a governess.

So while she knew she should be looking for another post, now that the last daughter, Lady Penelope, was safely married off, Miss Tibbles could not bring herself to do so. Instead she dithered.

As for the Earl of Westcott and his wife, the days stretched on and neither quite had the audacity to tell Miss Tibbles she must leave. After all, she had accounted for five daughters safely wed. To say they owed her a debt of gratitude was to grossly understate the matter!

And yet, as much as they respected her, the Westcotts undoubtedly found Miss Tibbles daunting and not the most comfortable of household companions. She had an unfortunate tendency to forget her place, you see, and to give, well, orders.

It was Lady Westcott's sister, Lady Brisbane, who hit upon the nacky notion of sending Miss Tibbles to Bath.

"We shan't take no for an answer," the Earl of Westcott said briskly as he told Miss Tibbles of the treat in store for her. "You deserve a holiday and why not? You shall go to Bath, take the waters, rest, and consider what you wish to do next. I have already arranged lodgings for you at a respectable place and paid ahead for the next two months. That ought to give you time to arrange matters to your satisfaction, should it not?"

Miss Tibbles stared at Lord Westcott, fully conscious of the generosity he was offering her. And all of the motives behind it. She had long known she was a woman who evoked respect but rarely liking in her employers. She understood only too well why they wished to be rid of her. And truth to tell, she was just as eager to be gone.

So now she forced herself to smile, albeit a trifle thinly, and say, "Thank you, Lord Westcott. It is most kind and generous of you and I am very grateful to you for thinking of such a thing."

"You will go, then?" he asked nervously. "The lodgings are paid for, any day you care to arrive."

Miss Tibbles correctly interpreted this to mean that the sooner she was gone, the happier the Westcotts would be. She did not blame them. As blue-deviled as she felt, she would not want to be around her either.

Aloud she said, "I shall be gone by the day after tomorrow."

Chapter 1

Bath. A quiet city that, if it had ever been truly fashionable, was now somewhat past that stage. A city which prided itself on respectability and propriety.

Rather like herself, Miss Tibbles thought wryly, as she stepped outside her lodgings, on her second morning in Bath, to take a walk.

It was not that she regretted coming. How could she, when the alternative would have been to take the first post, or at any rate, some post offered as governess?

There had been posts offered, of course. And Miss Tibbles had considered them. She had been able to imagine, only too clearly, the prospect of shaping yet one more unruly, rebellious, outrageous girl into a proper young woman. It is not surprising, therefore, that she had seized upon the opportunity for a holiday in Bath instead. Though what she could possibly find to do with herself here, aside from her daily walk, was rather beyond her.

After all, it was not as though the Master of the Pump would call upon a mere governess! Or that invitations to parties would come her way.

Still, it was better than the alternative.

Miss Tibbles suppressed a sigh and began walking in the direction of Milsom Street. Perhaps she could look in the windows of some of the wonderful shops or go to Hatchard's and find something to read to while away the afternoon hours. Perhaps, daring thought, if the weather stayed fine she could even read in the park!

So intent was Miss Tibbles on her thoughts, that she did not see the retired military gentleman until she crashed straight into him.

"I beg your pardon!" she gasped, turning bright red with mortification.

He smiled. His voice was brisk, accustomed to command she thought, as he said, "No, no, my fault entirely. I saw you and ought to have gotten out of your way. Colonel Merriweather, at your service, ma'am."

And what there was in that polite speech to make her color up even more, Miss Tibbles could not say. Indeed, she told herself tartly, she was behaving just as one of her silly schoolgirl charges might have done.

With an effort, she drew herself up straight, threw back her head, and said stiffly, "On the contrary, I was not watching where I was going so it was entirely my fault. However, I am grateful there was no harm done, to either one of us. Now if you will excuse me, sir, I am certain I am keeping you from some important appointment."

Miss Tibbles waited expectantly for him to go.

Colonel Merriweather stared at the woman before him and a mischievous devil set up his back. She was of scarcely medium height, slightly given to plumpness but not beyond what was pleasing. She was clearly past the first bloom of youth, but a nice-looking woman despite that. Her hair was almost completely hidden by her bonnet but her eyes were a deep blue that seemed almost to snap at him as she realized how he was perusing her.

Merriweather chuckled. So she had a spine, did she? Good. He couldn't abide missish creatures!

"I shall be happy to escort you wherever you are going," he said, offering her his arm.

"We have not been introduced."

He was certain she sniffed disdainfully as she said so. That roused his devil even more. Promptly he bowed. "Colonel Merriweather, retired. Late of His Majesty's forces on the Continent, where I was attached to the Duke of Wellington's staff in Paris. I am now retired and owner of a small estate not far from here. And you are?"

He thought she was going to turn and walk away. He thought she was going to refuse to tell him. Propriety dictated she snub him, after all, and from what he could see, the woman was entirely proper.

But perhaps she had a mischievous devil of her own, for just as Colonel Merriweather decided she was going to step around him, she said, in an oddly soft voice, "I am Miss Tibbles. Late of the post of governess to the Earl of Westcott's family."

Then, before he could speak to her again, she darted around him and hurried off down the street, as though that were the extent of her daring. Unless, he thought, drawing his eyebrows together in a frown, she thought he would not wish to know her once she told him she had been a governess. Or as if she were afraid of him.

He stared after her, turning her name over and over in his mind. It seemed oddly familiar. As if he had heard it before, but not for some time. Gradually awareness dawned. He recalled a young soldier, his best friend, laughing and telling him about the young lady he meant to marry when he went back home. Merriweather also remembered a battlefield. Cannons booming in the distance. Blood everywhere. His best friend dying in his arms. His last words a woman's name on his lips. "Marian. Marian Tibbles."

Abruptly Colonel Merriweather began running down the street after Miss Tibbles, calling out her name. After all these years, he had a message to give her, a duty to carry out. And he was dashed if he would allow a fear of looking foolish, or the risk of anyone watching, to stop him from doing so. It was a task which was long overdue.

"Miss Tibbles! Wait! I've a message for you!" he said, as soon as he was close enough that he thought she would be able to hear him.

The woman stopped. She turned and glared at him in outrage. She drew herself up to her full height. "Sir, you can have nothing to say to me, or I to you!"

Without waiting for his answer, she turned away and began to walk again, her pace a trifle quicker now as she hurried to get away from him. Merriweather did the only thing he could think of. He said, in a voice meant to carry to her ears only, "Marian."

She heard him. She halted. Stiffened. Slowly, incredulously, turned to look at him. "What did you say?" she asked.

He closed the short distance between them. Still keeping his voice pitched very low he said, "I called you Marian. That is your name, is it not?"

She started to speak, then stopped. She looked him up and down, a puzzled expression on her face. "I do not think I know you," she said slowly, "but apparently I am mistaken. Will you kindly refresh my memory, sir, as to precisely where and when we have met before? And the circumstances under which you came to think you had the liberty to use my name like that?"

He smiled. He couldn't help himself. She was pluck to the backbone, this woman, and he began to understand why his friend had admired her so dearly.

"We have never met," he admitted gently. At her frown he hastened to add, "I know of you only through Freddy Carrington."

Now she went very pale, and swayed. He reached out a hand to steady her. Her voice was scarcely above a whisper as she said, "He died over twenty years ago!"

"I know. I was there," Colonel Merriweather agreed,

speaking even more gently than before. "We were friends. He spoke of you often. Your name was on his lips as he lay dying."

That seemed to somehow give her strength. She abruptly realized his hand was on her arm and she stared at it pointedly. Colonel Merriweather let go.

She drew a breath and only someone standing as close to her as he was, would have been able to see her agitation. "That was a long time ago," she said, trying to speak in clipped accents and failing miserably. "Water under the bridge. What he may or may not have felt is irrelevant to me now."

"Is it?" the colonel countered, quirking an eyebrow upward in patent disbelief.

Some of the defiance left her shoulders. "No, of course not," she admitted. "I thought I had grieved for him and was over and done with it long ago, but I see that I am not. You are right, I should like to hear about Freddy Carrington. And how he died. I never knew, you see, beyond that it was in the middle of a battle."

"Did none of his friends come and tell you?" the colonel asked, curious. "I tried, when I was next in England, but I couldn't find you."

She looked everywhere but at him. She could not meet his eyes as she said, "Papa would not let any military men cross the threshold. And while I might have sought them out, after Papa died, I could not bring myself to do so. It was a difficult time and I had had too much of death. I could not bring myself to form any sort of acquaintance, even the slightest, with anyone who might be sent back to war and killed as Freddy, as Mr. Carrington was."

Despite himself, Colonel Merriweather was both touched and amused. "Surely some of them had already sold out," he pointed out, "and were therefore no longer in danger of getting themselves killed."

She surprised him, then. She did meet his eyes as she

said fiercely, "It didn't matter. I didn't wish to have anything to do with war and the military or any man who had ever had anything to do with either one!"

He answered not her words but the patent anguish behind them. He offered her his arm again as he said, quietly, "Come, let us find a place where I can get you a cup of tea. I'll tell you what I remember about Freddy Carrington and you shall ask me any questions you wish. And when we are done you may tell me to go to the devil and I shall."

She smiled at that, as he hoped she would. She even, after another moment's hesitation, took his arm. And together they set off down the street.

"Do you know where an inn might be found nearby?" he asked.

Startled, she shook her head. "I am only newly arrived to Bath. I was here once before, years ago, but I was a child then and remember very little. I thought perhaps you might know?"

He smiled and shook his head. "I am newly arrived myself. I came to visit my aunt and no doubt she knows but I did not think to ask her before I left the house. Ah, well, I am certain we shall find something. Heaven knows there are enough such places in this town."

Before he could say more, he was hailed by an acquaintance. Major Peter Hainesly was a sad rattle, but Merriweather knew him well and could scarcely pretend not to recognize the fellow. With an inward sigh, he introduced him to Miss Tibbles.

If he was afraid she would be daunted by the lively comments Hainesly threw her way, Merriweather was mistaken. She seemed almost in her element as she drew herself up, cast a withering glance at the fellow, and said, dryly, "How amusing. Do you always make it a point to offer Spanish coin to ladies past the point of believing such nonsense?"

But Hainesly was not daunted either. Too many set-downs came his way for him to care about one more.

"Tish, tosh," he said, waggling his fingers at her. "Ought to pretend you believe me, even if you don't." Then, to Merriweather he added, "Who the devil is this lady, anyway? Don't believe I've met her before and I've met almost every lady in Bath."

Colonel Merriweather thought he heard Miss Tibbles say, under her breath, "That I can well believe!"

He choked back a laugh. With creditable restraint he replied, "That is because Miss Tibbles is newly come to Bath, Hainesly."

But that would not do for her. She insisted on adding, looking Hainesly straight in the eye, "And because I have been, I am, a governess."

That startled the major. "A governess?" he repeated incredulously. To Merriweather he said, "What the devil are you doing with a governess in tow? You don't have any children. Do you?"

Now Merriweather did openly sigh. "No, Hainesly, I don't," he agreed. Then something prompted him to add, "I knew Miss Tibbles' fiancé some years ago. You remember Freddy Carrington, don't you?"

"By Jove, I do!" the major exclaimed. Now he looked at Miss Tibbles with a different, more careful eye and his voice was almost reverent as he said, "You don't mean to say this is Marian?"

Miss Tibbles colored up, becomingly in Colonel Merriweather's opinion. One she apparently did not share because she said tartly, "I pray you will not make the entire street a present of my name, Mr. Hainesly. Yes, my given name is Marian. But that life was many years ago. It is some time since I have thought of myself as anything except Miss Tibbles."

She was trying to put Hainesly, she was trying to put all of them, in their proper places, Colonel Merriweather thought. To remind them of what she conceived as the difference in their stations. He would not let her do it. He could not. For Freddy Carrington's sake.

Aloud he said, "Well, then, perhaps Major Hainesly and I ought to try to remind you of what it was like to be a much sought-after young lady."

He meant to jolly her. He meant to make her smile or even laugh. Instead, to his horror, Colonel Merriweather saw something suspiciously like tears gather in her eyes. And when she spoke, there was patent mortification in her voice.

"As a governess, one becomes accustomed to having to fend off unwanted attentions. One becomes accustomed to gentlemen presuming one is fair game. I had not thought to have to fear such a thing from Mr. Carrington's friends."

Both Merriweather and Hainesly recoiled in horror.

"No, here, not what I meant at all! Not what the colonel meant!" Hainesly insisted.

"We only meant," Merriweather said gently, "that to us you will always be the woman Freddy Carrington loved. Whatever your circumstances have been since then."

She went very still. Then a small laugh did escape her. "I have been very foolish," she said. "Chalk it up to the shock of hearing his name after so many years."

Colonel Merriweather patted her hand awkwardly. "You will feel much better, once you've had some tea," he said. He looked at Major Hainesly and explained. "Care to come with us?" he asked reluctantly.

Hainesly shook his head. "Can't abide tea. No, no, you two go. Wish you the best, and all that, Miss Tibbles. But I've an appointment. Already late. Must be going."

And Colonel Merriweather felt a curious lightness in his chest as he realized he was going to get to be alone with Miss Tibbles after all. Still, he did not so far forget himself that he did not gently steer her out of the way as two raggedy children came dashing down the street and nearly bowled her over.

"I think we had best find a place where I can procure you some tea," he said again.

She nodded, as though she did not trust herself to speak, and Colonel Merriweather could not blame her. It must have been, as she said, most unnerving to hear about Freddy after so many years.

Fortunately, they found an inn without too much difficulty and Colonel Merriweather bespoke a private parlor. When it looked as if Miss Tibbles might object, he said softly, "I cannot think you will wish to be an object of vulgar curiosity, as you might be if you should find yourself overcome by emotion when we speak of Carrington."

She nodded and made no further objection. When they were settled in the private parlor, he began.

Chapter 2

Miss Tibbles knew very well that it was not the thing to be alone with a gentleman, in a private parlor of an inn, but she could see no alternative. She did wish, how dearly she could not have known until this very moment, to hear about Freddy. And despite all her intentions otherwise, she knew she would indeed be overcome by emotion. Emotion that would make her, as the colonel had said, an object of vulgar curiosity if they were in the public parlor.

Besides, she thought, straightening her shoulders, surely she was past the age of needing to worry about a chaperon? Had she not performed that task herself frequently over the past eighteen years? Who would dare to question what she considered proper?

As for whether it was wise, something inside told Miss Tibbles that she could trust Colonel Merriweather. She had long ago learned to trust her instincts. She had learned that they were remarkably reliable.

So now she made small talk until the tea had been brought in. The colonel seemed to understand and spoke lightly of unimportant matters as well. But at last the tea had been set out and they were alone.

At the colonel's invitation, Miss Tibbles poured tea for both of them, then grasped her cup tightly. Indeed, she grasped it so tightly that she was afraid she would cause it to shatter and after one sip set down the cup and placed her hands in her lap instead.

In a voice that only shook a little, Miss Tibbles said, "Tell me about Mr. Carrington. Tell me how Freddy died."

The colonel looked at her, and she thought she saw pity in his eyes. But she didn't want that. She drew in her breath to tell him so and he forestalled her.

Suddenly there was, or seemed to be, a distinct twinkle in his eyes as he said, "You must think me lacking in wits for not answering you right away. It is just that Carrington was so good with words! He captured you to the life, with his description of you."

It was true, Freddy had been good with words. And because it was painful to remember that, Miss Tibbles straightened and said, tartly, "I scarcely think so, unless you are saying Freddy was prescient. I am now twenty years older than when Mr. Carrington knew me and circumstances have shaped my character more profoundly than I should think anyone could have guessed."

That ought to have put the colonel in his place, but it didn't. Instead he slowly shook his head and said, with a hint of a smile, "Not in the fundamentals, Miss Tibbles. You have the very strength of character Carrington talked about. He used to say you would make an admirable soldier's wife, for you were the one woman he knew who would be able to follow the drum and not be daunted by it!"

Miss Tibbles drew in her breath again. "He never said so to me."

There was hurt in her voice and the colonel seemed to sense it. He shook his head and told her gently, "He wouldn't have. Not Carrington. He was determined that you should never have to follow the drum. He didn't wish you to suffer the least inconvenience, if he could prevent it."

Thinking of her life, as it had been these past eighteen years since her father died and she had been on her own, Miss Tibbles was tempted to answer tartly. For those years had been full of inconveniences. But what would have been the point to that? Instead she said, "How did he die? Oh, I know it was in battle, but that is all I know."

Colonel Merriweather looked away, then back at her. The laughter in his eyes had been replaced by more than a hint of bitterness.

"Uselessly!" he spat the word. Then, recollecting to whom he was speaking, the colonel seemed to forcibly draw himself together and answer more completely.

"We were stationed in the West Indies. We thought it half a joke, at first. There was little fighting, except by some rebels, and we felt safe at the fort. Then the yellow fever began. It laid us low, so many of us. And the death toll was horrendous. Freddy was one of the first to succumb. And one of the first, one of the few, to rise from his sickbed to help care for the others and to go back to active duty. There were few real battles and boredom killed as many as fighting. Maybe it killed Carrington. When he heard the local militia were going to be sent to deal with some rebels in the hills, he volunteered to go along. And I went with him. We even took a cannon or two to try to destroy the rebels' stronghold."

He paused and there was a faraway look in his eyes. Miss Tibbles dared not break the spell that seemed to allow him to relive that day all over again, now. After a moment he went on.

"There was smoke. And cannons firing. Freddy and I were rallying opposite ends of the line of militia. We won. At least I think we did. And with very few dead on our side. But Freddy was one of them. When I found him, he was propped up on one elbow, trying hard to get to his feet. But he knew he was dying. The moment he saw me he said that I must tell you he was sorry. That he meant to come back to you and would have if he could."

The colonel paused and looked at Miss Tibbles. Somehow she managed to choke out the words, "I know that he would. He always kept his promises—if he could."

Colonel Merriweather nodded and then went on, "I wanted to get Freddy back to the fort, but he died right then and there. Your name—Marian—was on his lips with his very last breath. He must have loved you very much."

It was half a question and yet it wasn't. Marian felt her eyes fill with the tears she so deeply despised. She felt her hands twist together in her lap. She felt the colonel's concerned and gentle eyes on her face, though she could not bring herself to look up at him. Instead she began to speak, her own gaze locked on a faraway time and place.

"The last time I saw Freddy, I begged him to sell out. He looked so handsome in his uniform but I didn't care! I wanted him home, safe, with me. I wore my finest gown to try to tempt him. After he died, I burned it, to my father's complete bewilderment.

"He promised, that day, that he would sell out. Eventually. After he had made his mark. In his last letter to me, the one that arrived after he must have already been dead, Freddy said he had grown discouraged. That he meant to sell out, after all, in a few months. And then he would return to England and we would be married. He asked me to be patient only a little longer."

Colonel Merriweather nodded stiffly. "He meant it, too," he said gruffly. "We were used to roast him that he was falling prey to a woman's megrims, talking of selling out such a short time after he purchased his commission. But he was adamant. Said that he felt worse than useless where he was. And that the woman waiting behind for him, Miss Marian Tibbles, was worth any amount of roasting, any day."

Now the tears did spill out over her cheeks and Miss Tibbles swiped at them angrily with her gloves, but they would not seem to stop. Somewhere on her person, she carried a handkerchief, but for the life of her, at the moment, Marian could not remember where.

Suddenly she felt a handkerchief pressed into her hand and she used it gratefully. "I am very sorry to subject you to such a ridiculous display of nerves," she said, not daring to meet his gaze.

But he would not have it. A strong hand clamped over hers and that forced her to look up at him. There was a fierce expression on his face. "Never dare to apologize for caring!" he commanded her. "Do you think I should like it better if it seemed you could shrug off Carrington's death easily?"

"But it was such a long time ago," Miss Tibbles said helplessly. "Surely I should have outgrown my grief by now, sir?"

Now the fierceness left his face, to be replaced with a kindness, a gentleness, an understanding that was even more unnerving.

"You have not heard before how he died, and therefore it brings back the grief as fresh as if it were yesterday. That you have a heart able to care confirms every good thing Freddy ever said about you."

Marian blinked. She felt a warmth run through her that had nothing to do with the cloak she wore. She pulled her hand free, abruptly aware of how scandalously familiar she was allowing the colonel to behave. To be sure, it was perfectly understandable, she told herself, but no one seeing them would have known so.

She tried, desperately, to change the subject. To divert the colonel from looking at her in such a way. To allow herself some time to regain her composure.

"Please tell me about yourself," she said. "I collect you stayed with the military, all these years?"

He nodded. She felt rather than saw the action as he answered, "I have been in uniform for almost twenty-three years. Right up until a few months ago, when I sold out. It is all I have ever done, all I ever wanted to do."

"What will you do, now that you have sold out?" Marian prodded.

He hesitated and seemed to be searching for the right words to answer. Finally the colonel said, "I recently inherited an estate. I shall go there and place it in order. I simply came to Bath to visit my aunt first. And you? You said you are a governess? How did that come to be? Or ought I not to ask?"

She hesitated. But then what did it matter? Miss Tibbles asked herself. She met his eyes squarely as she said, "My father lived beyond his means. And he placed his faith in scoundrels. After he died I was told there was no money for me, nothing left after all his debts were paid. I had to find a way to support myself and I became a governess."

The colonel's eyes were grave as he asked, "Had you no relatives to turn to? No one who could offer you a home, instead?"

This was becoming harder by the moment! Marian bit her lower lip then forced herself to answer. "My father was not on the best of terms with his family. He had a knack for alienating everyone who might have cared about him. Who might have cared about me. After he died, I had no choice but to make my own way."

"I see." Miss Tibbles had the oddest feeling that perhaps he did. He was kind enough not to offer her pity and instead asked briskly, "I suppose you are with your charges, here in Bath and this is your afternoon free?"

Now it was Marian's turn to hesitate. "No, I, that is, in my last family, the youngest girl was finally married and I was no longer needed. My employers were kind enough to pay for a visit to Bath for me. I have a little time before I must find another post."

But it was not in her nature to speak in such an uncertain way and she forced herself to sit up straighter. "Indeed, I shall be looking for another post almost at once," she said briskly.

"But meanwhile, perhaps you will allow me to show you around, or rather, perhaps you will help me find my way around Bath?" the colonel asked. "I should be very glad of your company."

Miss Tibbles hesitated. She ought not to agree. It really was not entirely proper, not when their circumstances were so different. Not when they were, neither of them, related or married. But then, she had already had tea with him in a private parlor and that was not entirely proper either.

He seemed to understand because he said, quietly, "We are out of place, you and I, here in Bath. But I think it would not be so lonely if we had each other's company. I promise not to intrude on your thoughts. If you wish, I shall be entirely silent by your side. But it would give me pleasure to spend a little time with the woman Freddy Carrington regarded so highly. I think he would have liked us to do so."

Miss Tibbles ought not to listen to such words. But she did. Indeed, she looked up at Colonel Merriweather with a hint of something no one had seen in her eyes before, at least not for twenty years, as she said, "Perhaps we could spend this afternoon together, at any rate, though I do not know Bath any better than yourself. As I said, the last time I was here, I was but a child and I remember very little."

"Capital!" He beamed at her, brushing aside her caveat. "The same is true for me and we shall discover, or perhaps I should say, rediscover the city together."

Marian felt herself positively bask in the warmth of his

approval. She had always thought the expression a ridiculous one, but now she understood. And it wasn't so ridiculous after all.

The colonel rose to his feet. Marian rose to hers. And when he held his arm out to her, she took it. If a thousand eyes regarded her with censure, she still would have taken his arm. For one afternoon, she was not going to care what anyone thought. She was not going to play craven to propriety. And that was more shocking than anything that had yet been said or done between them.

Chapter 3

Miss Tibbles took off her bonnet and set it gently on the bed, back at her lodgings. She had had such a nice afternoon, spending it with Colonel Merriweather as they walked all over Bath and he told her more about his memories of Freddy. He had been all that was courteous, all that was kind, and he had even promised to call on her again. But of course that was mere politeness and she must not expect to hold him to such a promise.

When all was said and done, he was a retired military gentleman who had inherited an estate and she was a mere governess. No amount of kindness, on his part, could change that.

To be sure, it had been nice to pretend for one afternoon, to be a lady again. But Miss Tibbles had not survived the collapse of her world, eighteen years before, by giving herself over to daydreams. She had survived by making full use of her practical turn of mind. It was one thing to enjoy the kindness of Colonel Merriweather for one afternoon, quite another to allow oneself to be so foolish as to wish for another just like it.

Briskly, to remind herself of how different their lives were, Miss Tibbles sat down to write a courtesy note to Lord and Lady Westcott thanking them again for their generosity and to let them know, as they had asked her to do, how she liked the accommodations that had been arranged for her.

Even had it been the meanest hovel, Miss Tibbles should have been obliged, of course, to pronounce herself well satisfied. But in fact the lodgings were quite comfortable, located in a convenient part of Bath, and suited perfectly to her tastes.

It ought to have, therefore, been an easy letter to write. It was not. Miss Tibbles kept remembering when her father brought her to Bath and they hired a house in Rivers Street. They had walked past the house, she and the colonel, and it was amazing how much bitterness remained in her breast over the difference in her circumstances, then and now. Of course she had said nothing to Colonel Merriweather. Nevertheless, the bitterness was still there.

Indeed, it was just this bitterness that led Miss Tibbles to do something very, very foolish. When the letter was written and sanded and ready for the post, she snatched up her bonnet and headed back out the door.

Two hours later, Miss Tibbles returned, the proud owner of a new dress. Or rather, she would be, once the alterations were done. She was by turns defiant, proud, fretful, appalled, and wistful. For she had chosen a dress that could not, by any stretch of the imagination, be considered appropriate for a governess.

And yet, she could not entirely regret the act. Perhaps it was being reminded of whom she once had been. Perhaps it had been the flattering attention of a gentleman. Whatever the reason, Miss Tibbles had defied her cautious nature and ordered a dress made of a soft rose-colored silk, cut flatteringly low, designed to be worn while one waltzed in the arms of the man one loved.

Or so the modiste had fancifully said. Miss Tibbles would not allow herself to acknowledge that perhaps it was those very fanciful words which had, in the end, persuaded her to purchase the dress. She was, after all, Miss Tibbles and had a reputation to uphold!

A reputation that was very difficult to recall when, just as she was about to climb the stairs to her room, the landlady informed Miss Tibbles that a posy of flowers had arrived for her. For just a moment, Miss Tibbles allowed herself to remember what it felt like to be a girl receiving gifts from an admirer.

Then, briskly, she said, "Thank you, Mrs. Stonewell. No doubt they are a thank you from a former pupil. Or her parents."

"The card said that it was from a Colonel Merriweather," the landlady said slyly.

There might be a blush staining her cheeks but Miss Tibbles was not going to give her landlady the satisfaction of seeing she had discomposed her. Fixing Mrs. Stonewell with precisely the sort of quelling stare that always worked so well with her charges, Miss Tibbles said, coldly, "Yes. A friend of the family."

Precisely which family, she told herself as she climbed the stairs, there was no need for Mrs. Stonewell to know. Upstairs, however, she could not hide from herself the truth that she was more than a little touched and pleased that the colonel had sent her the posy. It was a thoughtful gesture and he was patently a thoughtful man.

For just a moment, Miss Tibbles allowed herself to wistfully imagine that there was room for, that it was possible to contemplate, at least a brief bit of romance in her life. And in that moment, she knew, without a doubt, why and for whom she had bought the dress. It was such a pity that he would never see her wear it.

Across town, Colonel Merriweather dressed for dinner, humming to himself as he did so, to the patent consternation of his valet. It would be too much to say that the colonel had been chafing at having to dance attendance upon his aunt in Bath, for he was genuinely fond of her, but there was no doubt that the boredom which had gripped him since his arrival was now gone.

And all because of Freddy Carrington's fiancée.

Merriweather frowned at that. He didn't like remembering that Miss Tibbles had been betrothed to another man, even if it had given him an excuse to speak to her further. He liked to think that even without it, he would have found a means to do so.

"They will be waiting for you," the batman who served as his valet said impatiently.

That brought Merriweather back to the present. He grinned at his valet. "And you think I ought to be down there? Well, quite right. I am very fond of my late uncle's wife, but she does not like to be kept waiting. Very well, this neckcloth shall have to do."

The batman grinned in return. "As if you don't always look top of the trees, Colonel."

Merriweather clapped his batman on the shoulder and headed for the door. He wondered if his aunt had ever heard of Miss Tibbles. And whether she could or would tell him anything about the woman.

Lady Merriweather was happy to see her late husband's nephew taking an interest in a woman. Of course she was. It was time, she had told Andrew more than once, that he married again and set up his nursery. Still, it was rather sudden, wasn't it, this interest in someone here in Bath? Or was she the reason he had come in the first place?

He smiled, charmingly in Lady Merriweather's opinion. "Oh, no. I had no notion Miss Tibbles was here. I had never met her but she used to be betrothed to one of my friends, before he died in battle," the colonel said carelessly. "I ran into her, quite literally, here in Bath today. I was just curious to know if you had ever met her."

"Miss Tibbles." Lady Merriweather turned the name

over in her mind, even as she spoke it out loud. "The only Miss Tibbles I have heard of," she said at last, "is a woman who was employed as a governess by my dear friend Lady Brisbane. Or rather, Lady Brisbane's sister, Lady Westcott. But surely that cannot be whom you mean."

When he did not at once answer, Lady Merriweather peered at her nephew more closely. "You do mean it!" she exclaimed in shocked tones.

This would not do. It would not do at all, Lady Merriweather vowed silently. Letters would need to be written, steps taken. At once! Of all her late husband's relatives, Andrew was the one she had the greatest fondness for and she could not stand by and let him make a fool of himself over some woman.

As though he could read her mind, the colonel reached out and took her hand in his. "Please. Don't," he said. "You do not know her background but I assure you it is quite respectable. Surely she is not to blame for the errors her father made? Surely you would not judge her without at least meeting her?"

Lady Merriweather liked to think she was a kind woman. She liked to think she was a fair one. And Andrew was looking at her with such a mixture of fondness, hope, and anxiety in his eyes that she could not bear to disappoint him.

"Very well," she said, very much against her better judgment. "I will meet this Miss Tibbles. And then decide. But I give you fair warning that on the face of it, I do not like this connection. I do not like it at all."

He kissed her hand, grinned that cocky grin that was so very hard to resist, then escorted her in to dinner. Cordelia Merriweather almost found herself hoping she would be able to like Miss Tibbles after all. Even though she was sure the woman must be after dear Andrew just because she wished to better her position. And even if she did not, even if she was not a grasping harpy, how could Cordelia wish for such a connection for him? A governess!

He might not have a title, but he did have a snug little estate to his name and could do much better for himself if he only tried. Cordelia would be happy to help him!

Lady Merriweather suppressed a moan as she recalled her plans to do just that. What was Lady Galworthy going to say if she could not persuade her nephew to call upon Lady Galworthy's daughter?

Looking over at Andrew, Cordelia was more certain than ever that he could read her mind. He grinned unrepentantly and said, confirming her worst fears, "I told you not to go matchmaking for me. I am happy as a widower. Set in my ways. I am not interested in getting married again."

Cordelia gasped, forgetting the servants in the room. "You mean to give the woman a slip upon the shoulder. Or a carte blanche?"

Now all trace of humor was gone from his face. "Don't be ridiculous," he snapped. "I mean to do nothing of the sort. I only asked if you knew anything about her. She is an acquaintance, nothing more. You really must stop reading greater meaning into everything I say."

Since she knew herself to be on very treacherous ground here, Lady Merriweather attacked her food as though nothing could possibly be of greater interest to her. To her vast relief, Andrew did not pursue the matter. Instead he talked of something else.

Until dessert. As Cordelia tasted her trifle, thinking that it really was her very favorite dessert, Andrew's voice shattered her composure.

The last of the servants had withdrawn and he regarded her over the rim of his wineglass as he said, his voice both stern and serious, "I meant it, Aunt Cordelia. I love you dearly but I shall turn tail and run from here as fast as I can if I discover you have been matchmaking for me."

Lady Merriweather was no coward. She met his gaze, tilted up her chin, and said, defiantly, "If you do not have a care for your interests, those of us who love you must do so. It is time you married again. And set up a nursery this time."

"Why?"

Cordelia almost gasped with outrage. "Because. You are above forty. How can you not want another wife. And children?"

"Very easily."

His voice was uncompromising. He was not, Cordelia thought bitterly, going to make this simple for her. That roused her own temper. "Very well, then, I shall tell you why you ought to care. You have a duty to produce an heir. You have never said so, but I can guess your first marriage was not a felicitous one. Well, then, this time listen to the counsel of your elders and perhaps you will do better."

To her consternation, he burst out laughing.

"Dearest aunt, I have an older brother. He has several children, among them three sons. He and his children are surely sufficient to guarantee the title continues. I need not add to the list. And as for my own estate, I should be perfectly happy to see it go to any one of his brats."

"Happy to leave it to one of them? Nonsense!" Lady Merriweather tried to look stern but sighed. "I truly do wish to see you happy, you know."

Now he was openly amused. "And you think it can only be so if I am leg-shackled? To some wife of your choosing?" he asked.

"Or of your own," she snapped. Then, although it was most improper, she reached across the table and put her hand over his. Her own voice was serious as she said, "You know how happy your uncle and I were together.

There is not a day that goes by when I do not miss him. I only wish for something of the same sort for you. It seems to me you did not have it with Drusilla and I had hoped, that once your year of mourning was over, which it now is, you would seek greater happiness with someone else."

He smiled at her then and lifted her hand to his lips. "Best of aunts, I am very glad my uncle found you," he said. "And I vow that if I found someone who could make me as happy as you made him, I should marry her in a shot."

Reluctantly, Lady Merriweather pulled her hand free. "You are roasting me," she said disconsolately. "You do not believe me when I say you would be happier if you were to wed again. Do you know, at this point I should even be happy if this, this governess were able to capture your heart. Not that I wish you to marry her," she added hastily, "for that would be absurd! No, I only wish that she could make you realize that there is something you are missing. Then you could look for a proper bride for yourself and we should all of us be able to stop worrying about you."

It was too much to expect that Andrew would listen with complacence and he did not. But when he rose and took his leave, saying he had promised to meet friends this evening, Cordelia at least felt that he might consider her words. She hoped so.

Meanwhile, perhaps she ought to invite Miss Tibbles to call on her. At a time when Andrew would not be about. Then she could judge for herself whether the woman was a risk or not.

But no, she would not take such a step without more evidence that Andrew was truly interested in the woman. Otherwise it would bestow far too much consequence upon a mere nobody who could not be trusted not to encroach upon the connection.

It was unfortunate that Miss Tibbles had come down so far in the world, but that was not Cordelia's problem. And indeed it would be a false kindness to encourage her to believe her circumstances might change so drastically that she and Cordelia could be intimates.

No, she was refining far too much upon words that Andrew had spoken no doubt just to tease her. Cordelia would, she decided, put the woman straight out of her mind unless or until Andrew forced her to do otherwise.

Except, perhaps, that she ought to write Lady Brisbane just to see what she had to say about the woman. It would have to be discreetly done, of course. For one thing, she did not wish to anger her nephew. And for another, she would not for the world expose him to the incredulous laughter of his peers should they learn he had expressed an interest in a governess!

Chapter 4

Miss Tibbles had no notion she was arousing such interest in Lady Merriweather's breast. Nor in anyone else's. To be sure, for the past several days, it seemed she encountered Colonel Merriweather almost everywhere she went. Of course, Bath was a very small city and it seemed he shared her love of reading, walking in the park, indeed simply walking. So perhaps it was not so strange, after all.

Miss Tibbles did not allow herself to contemplate the possibility that it was anything more than coincidence. She had learned long ago that it hurt too much to dream dreams which could not possibly come true.

Still, she found herself looking forward to seeing the colonel each day. If he was not at Hatchard's, she looked for him as she walked back to her lodgings. If she did not encounter him along the way, she found herself inclined to linger when she went for a walk in the afternoon. Without ever acknowledging to herself precisely why, of course.

The rose-colored dress now hung in her wardrobe and she stared at it wistfully every day, fingering the fine fabric as she did so. It was foolish beyond permission. She would never have an excuse to wear it. But neither could Miss Tibbles bring herself to regret one penny of the purchase.

Recollecting the dress, Miss Tibbles found herself

smiling, scarcely seeing where she was going. And suddenly there he was. Standing before her, smiling down at her as well.

"Colonel!"

His eyes twinkled as he said, with mock dismay, "What? Did you think I would fail you? How little faith you have in me. I am devastated."

That brought Miss Tibbles back to herself. "You are nothing of the sort," she retorted.

In answer, he drew her hand over and tucked it into the corner of his arm. They began to walk down the path as he said, conversationally, "Freddy Carrington used to say you had the most extraordinary sense of humor!"

Freddy Carrington. Miss Tibbles was astonished to discover that the grief she felt, the first day, when Colonel Merriweather had mentioned his name, was gone. It was replaced by an impatience to be done with speaking of someone who had been dead for some twenty years.

Appalled, Miss Tibbles could not bring herself to say so aloud. Indeed, the colonel seemed persuaded she still wore the willow for Freddy Carrington and had never gotten over her grief. She could not bring herself to disillusion him, for then he might not continue to talk to her each day. As dishonest as it was, she allowed him to continue to believe she wished to hear his stories of the time he had spent with Freddy Carrington in the military.

He thought he was telling her what an exceptional soldier Freddy Carrington had been. Instead, Miss Tibbles heard, in his words, what a remarkable officer Colonel Merriweather had been. She understood, though he was careful not to say so, that he had been concerned about the men he commanded, soothing fears the night before a battle, doing his best to bring as many back alive as possible, having a care for his fellow officers as well.

She knew without his saying so, that he had been at the side of every wounded or dying man, whenever possible.

She knew, by every word, by every line of his body, that Colonel Merriweather was a man whose life had been dedicated to his country, to the men who served with him, to protecting those left back home, to all the things that mattered.

Abruptly she realized he had stopped talking and was looking at her most expectantly. Miss Tibbles blushed, something she had been doing with alarming frequency, these past few days.

"I'm sorry, I was lost in thought," she admitted.

He took her hand, sending an odd tingling up her arm. "No, I am the one who should be sorry," he countered softly. "I ought to have realized how painful the memories would be for you, the grief that my words would bring back. Can you forgive me?"

She tried to pull her hand free. It was the proper thing to do. But he would not let it go, and short of causing a scene, there was no way to make him do so.

"There is nothing to forgive," she said.

Now he kissed her hand and then let it go and Miss Tibbles realized that she felt oddly bereft when he did so. Still, it was mere foolishness and she would not let it disconcert her. Or him.

Brightly she said, "Freddy Carrington must have been very grateful to have you for a friend."

Colonel Merriweather smiled, but as if her words brought him pain and she wondered why. His next words answered her question. "We were good friends. We both thought ourselves fortunate. And invincible. But we were not. In the end, I could not save him and he could not save himself. Perhaps, if I were a better friend, I could have done so. I have always felt as if a part of myself died when he did."

It was Miss Tibbles' turn to reach out to touch Colonel Merriweather. It was not strictly proper for her to do so, but at her age, what could it matter? Her reputation as a governess was too firmly established to be hurt by one small gesture. And the colonel looked as if he very much needed a kind touch.

"You have brought him alive again for me," she said.

Now his smile was deeper, even reaching his eyes. "If I have, then I am glad," he said.

There was a pause and Miss Tibbles self-consciously removed her hand from his arm.

"Perhaps, that is to say," the colonel began, as though he felt awkward, "Freddy Carrington loved music. He said you did as well. Perhaps you would do me the honor to attend a musical performance, in my company, tonight. In memory of Freddy Carrington, of course."

She ought to refuse. It would be most unwise to accept, feeling as she did, even in Freddy Carrington's name. If any of his friends were to see the colonel with her, he would be the subject of jests for some time for saddling himself with such an ape leader. She should refuse. She would refuse. Of course she would.

"I should love to go," she said.

He smiled and there was a new spring to his step as he made plans aloud. He told her what pieces were to be performed and what time he would call for her. He even spoke of arranging for a chair to carry her to the musicale.

It was at that point Miss Tibbles truly took alarm. "I pray you will not do anything so foolish, sir!" she protested. "I am scarcely an invalid and perfectly capable of walking such a short distance."

He looked as if he wished to insist, but he did not. Instead they talked a little longer, of other things, and he bowed over her hand as he took his leave of her, a short time later. Then Miss Tibbles was left to pass the rest of the afternoon as best she could.

It was difficult for she found the only thing she wished to do was think of Colonel Merriweather. And that could simply not be allowed!

* * *

If Miss Tibbles was disconcerted by what was happening, Lady Merriweather was even more so. Her letter had brought a swift reply from Lady Brisbane in London. If she was looking for a governess, Ariana had written, she could not do better! Miss Tibbles was an exemplary woman. She was proper and intelligent and strong-willed enough to handle the most difficult of girls. Was there some problem that Lady Brisbane had not heard of in the family?

Cordelia dropped the letter into her lap and sighed. There was a problem, but not the sort Lady Brisbane envisioned. The letter ought to have reassured her that Miss Tibbles had not set her cap for Andrew. The problem was, all the qualities Ariana described were precisely what would attract him to the woman.

As she was about to read the letter one more time, Andrew himself came into the room, fairly bouncing with good humor. "You must come to a musical performance with me this evening," he said, mischief in his fine gray eyes.

She distrusted that look. "I am not certain. That is to say, perhaps another night would be better?"

He came closer. "No," he said briskly, "it must be tonight."

"Why?"

"Because I have asked Miss Tibbles to go to the performance in my company. It will look better if you come as well and it will give you the chance to see for yourself what sort of woman she is."

"On the contrary, it will look most particular!" Lady Merriweather retorted, with some exasperation.

He reared back, then frowned. "Well? And what is wrong with that?"

"What is wrong with that is you will be making her the target of every malicious tongue in Bath!"

"Oh. Nevertheless, I really should like to have you come along as well," he said.

Lady Merriweather hesitated. And yet what choice did she really have? If someone didn't see the woman, speak to the woman, make it clear to her that it was best if she drew back and discouraged Andrew's attentions, who knew where these things might go?

"Very well, I shall come."

"Thank you, best of aunts!" he said, in great good humor. "You shan't regret it, I promise you."

"A great many men have said that to a great many women," she retorted tartly, "and somehow we always do."

But he could not be swayed from his good humor and that, Lady Merriweather feared, was the worst sign of all. Still, she had said she would go and she was not a woman to go back on her word.

Well, if anyone asked, she would say that she was being kind to the woman for Ariana's sake. And that her nephew was doing the same. It wouldn't scotch all the rumors but perhaps it would put a damper on the worst of them.

So thought Lady Merriweather, the optimist. Lady Merriweather the pessimist waited for disaster to fall.

Her first sight of Miss Tibbles, that evening, confirmed Lady Merriweather's worst fears. The woman was dressed in a gown of rose-colored silk that no governess should or would ever wear. And in it she looked much younger than she had been given to believe Miss Tibbles could possibly be.

But the worst of it was the way Andrew was gazing at her with such patent approval in his eyes. And the way she blushed so becomingly when he introduced her to Cordelia. It would have been better, far better, if she squinted, or was ten years older, or suffered from an arrogance of manner. That was the portrait painted for her by everyone who had ever met Miss Tibbles. Well, perhaps not the squint, but everything else. What on earth had happened to the woman?

Unfortunately, even as she asked herself the question, Lady Merriweather thought she knew the answer. Love.

Not that either Andrew or Miss Tibbles seemed aware yet, of how deeply their affections had become engaged. But it would happen, soon enough, she thought gloomily. And because it was evident that Miss Tibbles was not battening onto her nephew for personal gain, it would be all that much the harder to detach her from his company.

Mind you, Lady Merriweather admired anyone who could survive the disaster which had befallen Miss Tibbles' family and make something of herself as the woman had, but that did not mean that Cordelia could contemplate a connection with her nephew with any sort of complacency.

She set out to make this clear to Miss Tibbles.

"My dear, I have heard a great deal about you," Lady Merriweather told Miss Tibbles with a polite smile.

"Indeed?"

Good, she had a cautious air about her. That meant she must already know how precarious this all was. Lady Merriweather allowed her smile to deepen.

"Yes. You must know that Lady Brisbane is a particular friend of mine and I know how she and her sister have treasured your services."

Miss Tibbles blanched. Cordelia almost felt sorry for the woman, but it was best that matters were made clear right from the start.

"Yes, Lady Brisbane tells me that you are on a short holiday but will be hiring out again very soon. If you should need any help locating a family in need of your services, I pray you will let me know and I shall be happy to help you find a new post."

There, that should make matters clear to the woman,

Lady Merriweather thought with some satisfaction. Unfortunately, it also made her position clear to Andrew.

There was patent anger on his face as he moved closer to Miss Tibbles. "There will be no need for her to rush into a new position," he said curtly.

But that was too much for Miss Tibbles. Apparently she did not like having someone champion her. She tilted up her chin even as she moved a step away from Andrew. Lady Merriweather strongly approved. She also met Cordelia's gaze firmly even as she spoke directly to Andrew.

"Actually, Lady Merriweather is quite correct. I shall have to seek a post soon. The Westcotts have been generous enough to pay for two months' lodgings for me, here in Bath, but no more than that."

She was reminding Andrew, and perhaps herself, of how things stood. Cordelia admired her for it and under other circumstances would have liked Miss Tibbles very well. A pity the connection could not be encouraged. She would have given a great deal to see him look at an eligible young lady the way he was looking at this governess.

Someone like Daphne Galworthy who was, Cordelia realized, headed straight toward them, along with her mother. Lady Merriweather closed her eyes, sent up a silent prayer, then fixed a welcoming smile upon her face as she turned toward her friend.

"Emily! How delightful to see you here! And Daphne is in such looks tonight. Do you not think so, Andrew?"

Thus appealed to, he had no choice but to be polite. "Lady Galworthy. Miss Galworthy."

His bow was the precise degree required and no more. His voice was sufficiently cool to discourage lingering, but not so cold as to be rude. Cordelia could have slapped him for it. Particularly when Lady Galworthy looked past them to Miss Tibbles and said, "Who is this, my dear? Your new companion, perhaps?"

There was no help for it. Miss Tibbles would have to be introduced. Lady Merriweather did so reluctantly. The only one who looked more unhappy than she felt was Miss Tibbles. As for Daphne, she scarcely listened. Instead she placed a hand on Andrew's arm and leaned toward him as she asked some question about his military service.

Really! The girl was most unbecomingly forward. In contrast, Miss Tibbles managed to convey by her manner, if not by her words, that she had approached Lady Merriweather to ask for help finding a new post.

Since this was precisely the tack Cordelia had already decided to take, she ought not to have felt annoyed, but she did so. After watching Daphne's reprehensible behavior with her nephew, Cordelia actually found herself wishing she could give Lady Galworthy and her daughter a setdown by making it clear that Andrew had asked Miss Tibbles to come tonight because he enjoyed her company.

How had she ever thought Daphne Galworthy would do for Andrew? That was the soft question he asked her the moment the pair had moved out of earshot.

"Really, Aunt Cordelia! Could you not do better than that?" he demanded with that exasperatingly sardonic air of his.

"How was I to know the girl was so forward?" Lady Merriweather retorted defensively. "She has always behaved becomingly when I have seen her before."

He sighed. "Please, Aunt Cordelia, I know you mean it for the best but please stop matchmaking for me."

Her sigh echoed his own. Perhaps he had a point. If only he would find someone himself!

Fortunately Miss Tibbles appeared oblivious to what just had occurred. Either that or she had even better manners than Cordelia had given her credit for, if that were possible. It did not please Lady Merriweather. She didn't want to find anything to like about the governess. She didn't want to find anything to approve. Good heavens, at this rate, how was she possibly going to find the arguments to persuade Andrew to detach himself from her?

As a result, the only one who seemed to enjoy the evening was Andrew. And only because he got to sit very close to Miss Tibbles.

It was enough to give anyone the megrims.

Colonel Merriweather stared at Miss Tibbles and swallowed hard. She was not beautiful, in the way young girls like Miss Galworthy might be said to be beautiful. But in her dress of rose-colored silk, she looked beautiful to him.

She carried herself with a poise no young girl could hope to match. And there was such understanding in her blue eyes that he wanted to reach out and touch her face.

She wore her hair differently tonight and he could see that it was soft and curling and he wanted to touch that as well. But he couldn't. She was tolerant of him because he was able to tell her about Freddy Carrington but he could not believe Miss Tibbles would tolerate a familiarity from him beyond that.

Andrew almost swore. He didn't want her to see him as Freddy Carrington's friend. He wanted her to see him as clearly as a man as he saw her as a woman. He wanted Miss Tibbles to want to touch him.

But he could scarcely say such a thing to her. She would think he was trifling with her. As she had so bluntly given him to understand, that first day, other men had tried to trifle with her, trifle with the governess she had been, over the years.

She thought her years as a governess made her ineligible. He could see it in her eyes, in the way she carried herself, in the way she effaced herself when that dragon of a woman, Lady Galworthy, came over with her daughter. Andrew wished he knew the magic words to take away that image she had of herself. He wished he knew the magic words to allow Miss Tibbles to see herself as he did.

Instead he made it his business to help her feel it, by the way he asked her preferences, the way he looked after her comfort, the way he was swift to procure her, and his aunt of course, refreshments. And the way he let his hand linger a moment, holding hers, when he said good night.

It was sometime during that evening, Colonel Merriweather couldn't have said when, that he decided he was going to make Miss Tibbles his wife. He understood too well, however, that the *ton* would see it as a most unequal match and so he said nothing. Not to her. Not to his aunt.

If his years in the military had taught him anything, it had taught him that one did not attack until one had one's plan of action thoroughly mapped out. Until one had undertaken scouting expeditions and knew the terrain that lay ahead. Until one had chosen the proper place for battle.

Soon enough both Miss Tibbles and his aunt would know what he was about. But not just yet.

Chapter 5

Colonel Merriweather carried out his campaign as ruthlessly as any he had undertaken against Napoleon. He sent Miss Tibbles flowers. He continued to meet her almost every day. He ignored the jibes of friends. And he tried very hard to ignore the jibes of his own heart.

Perhaps he was mad. His aunt would certainly say so. Perhaps he should give Miss Tibbles more time, but he didn't know how much longer she would be in Bath. And, he told himself, they were neither of them growing younger. What might be foolish impulse in a green boy was merely, at his age, the ability to know his own mind and make decisions swiftly.

And so, the following Thursday, he nerved himself to speak to Miss Tibbles about how he felt. They were in the park, walking among the gardens, when he turned to her and said, "I am a military man. I know no other way to do this than by plain speaking."

Instantly a stricken look sprang into Miss Tibbles' eyes. Merriweather paused to take a breath and she spoke before he could go on.

"There is no need to explain further," she said, her hand creeping up to clutch at the top of her dress. "You have wasted more time than you can spare with me. I understand, fully, and beg you will not think twice about the matter. You have been more than patient with my questions and I am cognizant of your forbearing."

She paused for breath and this time it was Colonel Merriweather who leapt into the breach. "No! The devil take it, Miss Tibbles. Marian. I wish to tell you that my feelings for you are very strong."

"I—" She stopped from her evidently intended reply and blinked at him. "They are?" she whispered.

He nodded. "I know you are still pining for Freddy Carrington."

"No."

It was Colonel Merriweather's turn to be shaken. "You are not?" he asked.

She shook her head.

"Do you think, then, that it is possible you could come to care for me?" he asked, not caring that every anxiety he felt could plainly be read upon his face.

"I already do," she said.

He stared. He blinked. An incredulous smile lit up his face. Before he could stop to think about where they were or who might see, he reached for Miss Tibbles and kissed her warmly on the lips.

It was wrong of him. Most improper. Highly foolish in such a public place.

But he kissed her. He could not stop himself. And it was more than a moment before she tried to stop him. Instantly he let her go and stood back, feeling as shaken as she looked. He started to apologize. She started to speak. A third voice intruded, shattering the bubble of privacy their imaginations had conjured around them.

"Miss Tibbles!" a scandalized voice cried out.

Colonel Merriweather and Miss Tibbles both turned to look. A very elegantly dressed young lady was hurrying toward them, an appalled look upon her face. Behind her was a gentleman Andrew thought he recognized. The gentleman looked more amused than upset, but one look at Miss Tibbles was enough to tell Andrew they were in trouble.

"Miss Tibbles!" the young woman repeated, in tones of outrage, as she came up to them. "How can you behave so? And in such a public place! When I think of what you would have said to me had I behaved so improperly, why I cannot credit what I have just seen."

"Then don't," Merriweather said shortly.

The young woman turned to him and prepared to assault him with the full measure of her fury. "How dare you, sir? Miss Tibbles is a respectable woman! How dare you force your attentions on her?"

Andrew almost laughed. But the situation was too grave for that. He didn't know how to answer. But Miss Tibbles did. He could hear her draw in her breath and also draw herself up to her full height before she began to speak.

"His attentions were not forced, Lady Farrington!" Miss Tibbles said sternly. "And as for improper behavior, surely I taught you better than to run along a public path? Surely I taught you it was improper to raise your voice in public this way?"

For a moment he thought it would work. Then Lady Farrington began to shake her head. "Oh, no, Miss Tibbles. You won't cozen me like that," she said, taking a step forward. "I know what I saw. And it was most improper. Who is this man and why was he kissing you?"

"I can tell you that," the gentleman behind her said. "He is Colonel Merriweather. It is still 'Colonel,' is it not? How are you, Andrew?"

He grinned. "I thought I recognized you. You're Lord Farrington, now, aren't you? Come up in the world. Is this spitfire your wife?"

"Yes."

But this was too much for the young woman. She stepped between Merriweather and Farrington. Her dark eyes were snapping with anger as she said, "Very well, so now I know who you are, sir, but you still have not said why you were kissing Miss Tibbles. And in such a public place!"

It was Marian's turn to advance upon Lady Farrington. "Before you begin to lecture me," she said, "let me remind you, Lady Barbara, of a certain party game you took part in during your first Season in London. How many gentlemen was it who kissed you then?"

Now Farrington looked startled. "Party game?" he echoed. "Men kissed you?" he asked his wife, his expression beginning to darken.

"It was a game," she stammered. "No one thought anything of it. Everyone was playing. How on earth did you learn about that, Miss Tibbles?"

"Never mind that," Farrington countered, "what were you doing playing such a game in the first place?"

It was clear to Merriweather that far from being gratified, Miss Tibbles appeared to regret her hasty words. She touched Farrington's arm and said, "Really, I should not have said anything. It was a harmless game and it was true many girls took part in such things then."

Andrew looked from one to another and then back at Marian. He could not bear to see the distress on her face. Well, he knew how to create a diversion. He had done so often enough in battle.

Merriweather moved to stand beside Miss Tibbles and even put an arm around her waist. Defiantly he looked at Lady Farrington and said, "To answer your most impertinent question, though I cannot see why I should, Miss Tibbles and I are going to be married. And since we are, I do not see what affair of yours it is if I should choose to kiss my betrothed here or anywhere else."

That did it. A shocked silence fell over the four of them. The diversion had worked, although both Farringtons were regarding Andrew with some doubt. He looked to Miss Tibbles, expecting her to second his words. She didn't. Was she still distressed? he wondered. Embarrassed?

No, he realized, she was furious!

"How dare you presume so far?" she demanded, rising almost to her toes. She whirled and faced the Farringtons. "It is not your place to judge my behavior, Lady Barbara. But since you have I will allow that perhaps it was ill-advised. Particularly since I am not going to marry Colonel Merriweather. He is only saying so in an effort to salvage my reputation in your eyes. What he cannot know is that it needs no salvaging. Does it?"

It was not a question and Lady Farrington did not dispute the answer. There was a mulish set to her mouth, however, and before she turned on her heel, she said, "Very well, Miss Tibbles. As you say, it is none of my affair. But I am going to write Mama!"

And then she stalked away. Farrington stayed long enough to assure Merriweather, "I shall do my best to hold her in check."

"Thank you," Andrew said, and he meant it.

He watched as Farrington hurried to catch up with his wife and before they were out of sight or earshot, Andrew heard him ask her again about kissing games.

Then, to his relief, they were alone, he and Miss Tibbles. If one could call a public park alone. Particularly when there were, Andrew now realized, far too many interested eyes watching them. Conscious of that, he offered Miss Tibbles his arm. From her heightened color, he guessed that she accepted it for the same reason.

As they walked, he kept his voice pitched low as he said, "Forgive me. I should not have done that here."

"No," she agreed. "Nor told such a bouncer as that you and I were going to be married."

"It wasn't a bouncer," Andrew protested. "To be sure,

I hadn't quite meant to ask you just yet, but it was only a matter of time."

"Indeed?" Miss Tibbles stopped walking and turned to face him. "And you were so certain of my answer?"

Andrew stared at her, bewildered. "But you said you cared for me," he said.

"I do," she answered. "But what has that to say to anything? I may have forgotten myself for a moment, but only a moment. There can be no future, no marriage between us. And you must know it as well as I do."

"No, I do not!" Merriweather said with some exasperation. Then, deciding that it was time to take the offensive, he added, "Tell me, then, why there cannot be anything between us for I do not acknowledge it to be so. Convince me, though I am persuaded you will not be able to do so."

Now she could not meet his eyes. "Because. We are not of the same station. Not anymore. You are a gentleman. A landowner. I am a governess. Neither I nor anyone else will ever be able to forget that."

He shook his head. Slowly at first, and then with greater speed. "No," he said.

That startled her. "No?" she echoed cautiously.

"No. I will not let you destroy our happiness, before it has even begun, with such nonsense. If I do not care for any supposed difference between our stations, what right has anyone else to do so? You were a young lady and you will be a lady again, whatever has happened in between."

She stared at him, her jaw hanging open, as though she thought he had lost his wits. And perhaps he had. Certainly most of the *ton* would tell him so. But Colonel Merriweather knew what he wanted. And what he wanted was Miss Tibbles. So now he took her hands in his, gently, but refusing to let go when she tried to pull them free.

"Well," he asked softly, "will you marry me?"

* * *

He was mad. He must be mad. It was the only possible explanation. That was what Miss Tibbles told herself. Either that or Colonel Merriweather was roasting her. He could not possibly mean what he had just said.

And even if he did, even if she was tempted, just for a moment, to allow him to persuade her, she must recollect his family. And how distressed they would be if he made such a mésalliance. She could not let him do it. She must protect him from the consequences of his folly.

"No. I cannot marry you," she said, tilting up her chin high into the air.

"Why not?" he demanded promptly.

"What?"

"Why not?" he repeated. "Why can't you marry me? Are you married already? Ruined? Have a horrid distaste for men? What is it? We have already established that it cannot be a distaste for me in particular. And we have already established that any supposed difference in our stations is irrelevant. So why can you not marry me?"

It was grossly unfair that he should hold her so strictly to account, Miss Tibbles thought with exasperation. And grossly unfair that he should continue to hold her hands, stroking the backs of them with his thumbs. And even more grossly unfair that he should be looking at her with such kindness in his eyes. Kindness and something more. Something she had never thought to see again, after so many years, directed at her inconsequential person. Something that almost, almost persuaded her to set aside her principles and accept his offer.

But she could not do so. It would not be fair to the colonel.

Primly she said, still trying to ignore the feel of his thumbs stroking her hands, "This is absurd. I need not give you a reason. If you truly cared for me, you would simply accept my word."

He snorted. He said a rude word. Marian felt a sense of

panic running through her. How could she manage a man who would not listen to her? For eighteen years she had been a governess, and while it had not always been easy, for eighteen years she had been listened to. Well, generally. After she used a bucket of cold water or made a girl stand on one foot as she recited multiplication examples, the girl always listened. So what was she to do with someone like this?

If she could only have known, she would have discovered that Colonel Merriweather was feeling much the same. He had been an officer for too many years to bear thinking of. And he was accustomed to instant obedience to his orders. But he had the lowering sensation that Miss Tibbles was not likely to take orders very well.

Still, he could not help but persist. Perhaps a different approach was called for here? Softly, coaxingly, he said, "Please, Marian? I shall follow you about, you know, if you don't agree to marry me. I shall announce loudly, to all and sundry, that I mean to marry you, whatever you say."

With some asperity she said, "I shall not be browbeaten, Colonel Merriweather!"

"Yes, Marian," he said with a meekness that deceived neither of them. He saw a smile twitch at the corner of her mouth and he persisted. "I shall go into a terrible decline if you refuse me, you know."

Another twitch, at the other corner. She could not meet his eyes as she said, mournfully, "That would be a terrible thing."

"Yes, it would. And I think you would go into something of a decline as well, wouldn't you?" he asked, wishing she would look at him.

But Miss Tibbles kept her eyes firmly on the ground as she agreed, "Perhaps I would."

He lifted both hands, one after the other, to his lips and

kissed them. "Well, then? Will you not marry me? Or at least consider doing so?" Andrew added hastily as he felt her stiffen.

"I suppose I could consider the matter," she answered in a voice so soft he had to strain to hear her.

He would have let out a whoop of triumph. He would have pulled her into his arms and kissed her all over again.

At least he would have done so if he had thought she would allow it. But he decided it would be wiser to simply offer her his arm.

With only a little hesitation she took it. As they walked along the path he said, conversationally, "I shall have my aunt call on you. Or invite you to call upon her. She liked you, you know."

"Yes, as a woman," Marian replied tartly. "As your possible wife it is a different matter entirely. She will not be pleased."

Andrew wanted to disagree but he had a strong feeling she was right. Instead he said, lightly, "Well, if she is not pleased we must just set ourselves the task of bringing her around. It should not be too difficult. She dotes on me, you know."

"That is precisely why it will be all but impossible," Miss Tibbles retorted.

He shook his head. "Nonsense. Leave it all to me and I promise my aunt shall welcome you with open arms."

Andrew could not quite catch what Miss Tibbles muttered under her breath and he strongly suspected it was perhaps just as well if he didn't try.

Chapter 6

If Lady Merriweather did not welcome Miss Tibbles with open arms, she was at least kind. Honest but kind. She invited her to call, received her in the drawing room, and chatted amiably for some time with the governess. It was not until she offered Miss Tibbles money to leave Colonel Merriweather alone, however, that he realized what his aunt meant to do. That was when he lost his temper.

"Aunt Cornelia, you are speaking to the woman I intend to marry! If you do not wish a complete breach between us, you will treat her with respect."

Marian, for so he had begun to think of her, reached out a hand to stop him, but Andrew was too angry to temper his words. He began to pace about the room as he went on.

"Her birth was as respectable as my own," he told his aunt.

"Her father died bankrupt," Lady Merriweather countered.

"That is his mistake, not hers."

"She has been a governess."

"And I have been a colonel."

"She is too old to give you heirs!"

That brought Andrew to an abrupt halt. He looked at his aunt and then at Miss Tibbles, who looked as though she wished to be anywhere but here.

"Enough," he said in a voice that was quiet but accustomed to command. "It is my decision."

That roused Marian, as he knew it would. "On the contrary, Colonel Merriweather," she said indignantly, "it is my decision as well!"

He grinned, far preferring her anger to her embarrassment. "Yes, my love," he said meekly.

"Oh, very well, do whatever you wish," Lady Merriweather said petulantly. "You always do. But do not expect me to be pleased about it. And what your brother, who is now head of the family, will say, I do not like to think."

"Then don't," Andrew replied promptly. "Come, Marian, I think my aunt has abused you long enough."

He held out his hand to her but, to his consternation, she did not move.

Miss Tibbles stared at Andrew. She liked him. She truly did. But she was not about to let anyone order her about. And besides, however much she disliked it, the truth within Lady Merriweather's words still stung.

They were, after all, very little different from what she had been saying to herself, all along. So now she took a deep breath, looked over at Colonel Merriweather, who still held out his hand to her, and said, "No. Why do you not go for a walk and leave me to talk with Lady Merriweather alone."

He hesitated. He started to insist. Something in her level gaze stopped him. With lips pressed tightly together he stalked from the room.

Miss Tibbles found that she was holding her breath until he was gone. Then she turned to Lady Merriweather, who was regarding her with the oddest expression.

"Do you always treat him so?" Lady Merriweather asked. "I have never seen him listen to anyone before."

"Forgive me for doing so," Marian said, gathering her

courage. "I thought it would be best if we could speak frankly and it would not have been possible if he were still here. You said a great deal to him about me. It is nothing I have not said to myself. I quite agree with you, you see, as to why there should be objections to such a match."

"Then why are you still encouraging my nephew's attentions?" Lady Merriweather demanded coldly.

Miss Tibbles smiled wistfully. "Because I cannot help myself. Imprudent or not, I care for him. And because he will not listen when I try to discourage him."

For a long moment, Lady Merriweather did not speak. Then she said, almost to herself, "He is stubborn, I will grant you that. Still, it is not wise. On the other hand, you will not let him run roughshod over you. Something he is accustomed to doing. And it would be entertaining to watch. But no. It is a connection that would be condemned roundly. I fear I cannot give you my consent, Miss Tibbles."

Marian found herself regarding the other woman steadily. A demon of temper grew within her breast. She ought to meekly agree with Lady Merriweather. And she ought to meekly take her leave. But she didn't.

Instead Miss Tibbles rose to her feet and said, coolly, "I do not think consent is yours to either give or withhold, Lady Merriweather. I am very sorry it displeases you. But Andrew," she said, using his given name, knowing it would enrage her ladyship, "is of age. I do not think he will care a button. It is a pity we cannot be friends but fortunately I never deluded myself into thinking it could be so. Good day, Lady Merriweather."

And then she turned and walked calmly from the room. Behind her, Marian could hear Lady Merriweather murmur angrily and finally, goaded beyond restraint, call out, "I shall write Lady Brisbane about this! Yes, and all my other friends as well!"

Which, Miss Tibbles thought, with a lowering sensation as she began the walk back to her lodgings, might very well mean that she would not be able to find another post.

She ought to go back and apologize. She ought to swallow her pride and make peace with Lady Merriweather. Certainly she had done so with far more difficult women, her employers, over the past eighteen years. But somehow, today, she found she could not do it.

What she was going to do was a question Marian could not begin to answer. She only knew that she could not go back and tell Lady Merriweather that she regretted the feelings Colonel Merriweather had for her. And that was the only answer which would have appeased the woman.

So intent was Miss Tibbles on her thoughts that she scarcely noticed, when she reached her lodgings, a couple waiting for her in the parlor. She would have hurried up to her room had the landlady not stopped and told her.

"You've guests, Miss Tibbles. In the parlor."

From her landlady's respectful tone, Marian could only surmise that the guests were Quality. She wondered idly if Barbara had come to call and whether she meant to ring another peal over Miss Tibbles' head.

But it wasn't Barbara. Instead, in the parlor, Annabelle, dear sweet Annabelle, the second oldest of the Earl of Westcott's daughters, sat waiting with her husband, Lord Winsborough. Miss Tibbles hurried toward her.

"My dear! How delightful to see you! When did you arrive in Bath? How are the children?"

Shyly Annabelle hugged her former governess. "We arrived just last night," she said. "And wished to come and see you, straight away. Didn't we, David?"

Miss Tibbles turned to Lord Winsborough, who was smiling. There was a hint of something grave, however, at the back of his eyes. Still, his voice was kind as he said, "We did indeed, Miss Tibbles."

A little flustered by something in both their manners, she said hastily, "Pray, be seated. How long will you be in Bath? Where are you staying?"

Lord Winsborough did his best to answer while Annabelle kept darting odd glances at Miss Tibbles. With a sinking sensation, Marian realized they must have heard something about Colonel Merriweather and his interest in her. Was it possible, she wondered, that Barbara had already written them and they had come to Bath because of it?

Just as she was thinking of him, the landlady showed Colonel Merriweather into the parlor. He looked to be in something of a temper. The moment he saw she had guests, however, he put it aside and smiled as he stepped forward to greet them.

Marian was pleased to see that he did his best to put Annabelle at ease. She was a dear girl, but a trifle shy. Lord Winsborough watched Andrew with a steadiness that argued he had indeed heard something.

As the two men talked, Annabelle moved to sit beside Marian. Quietly she asked, "Is everything all right, Miss Tibbles?"

And how was she to answer that? "I am well," Marian said, cautiously.

Annabelle glanced over to Andrew. The two men were engrossed in their own conversation and she felt free to ask Miss Tibbles, "Is the colonel someone you have known for a long time?"

"I met him here, in Bath."

"But he is some sort of family friend?" Annabelle probed.

Suddenly Marian could stand it no longer. She had done nothing to be ashamed of and this tiptoeing about was foreign to her nature.

"Colonel Merriweather would not say so, though he

did know someone I knew, many years ago. I suppose you might say that he is courting me."

Annabelle gave an exclamation of delight that claimed the attention of everyone in the room. With some asperity Marian said, "You need not sound so delighted and you need not announce it to the entire household."

"But I am happy for you," she countered easily.

"May I ask what you are happy about?" Colonel Merriweather asked.

Both Annabelle and Miss Tibbles blushed at the question. One could not very well tell a gentleman, after all, that they had been discussing his courtship of a lady. Still, it was evident he had guessed.

"I hope you were trying to persuade Miss Tibbles to accept my suit," he told Annabelle. He paused and added, to Lord Winsborough, "I know it is not what the world would call an advantageous match for me, but it is one I dearly wish for. If only I could persuade Miss Tibbles I truly feel so."

"This is absurd!" Marian snapped. "I am quite old enough to know my own mind!"

"Positively ancient, in fact," Lord Winsborough said teasingly.

"Well past her last prayers," Annabelle chimed in, a sweet smile taking the sting out of her words.

"Old enough to know," Andrew said, taking her hand so that she did not know where to look, "that we have no time to waste. You know we are both only going to grow older, Marian. Why should we let slip away the time we have left?"

This was too much for Miss Tibbles. She pulled her hand free, rose to her feet, and began to pace about the room in patent agitation.

"You speak as though we truly were ancient! If that is what you think, Colonel Merriweather, I wonder that you will even consider a woman as old as myself! No, I will not be rushed. Not by you. Not by Annabelle or Lord Winsborough. Not by anyone."

"And no one shall make you, Miss Tibbles," Annabelle said firmly. "David and I shall protect you from anyone who would try."

Since Lady Winsborough's gaze was firmly fixed on Colonel Merriweather, there could be no doubt who or what she meant. He held up his hands in a gesture of surrender.

"I only want what is best for Miss Tibbles," he said meekly.

"What you think is best for me," Marian retorted tartly.

He glanced at her, a puzzled look upon his face. "So I said," he agreed.

"Did it never occur to you that you might be mistaken?" she demanded hotly.

He came closer, oblivious to the other two in the room. "Am I not to point out to you when you are mistaken in your thinking?" he asked.

She poised to tell him precisely what she thought of such a reply. But she had no chance. Before she could realize what he meant to do and stop him, Andrew had drawn Marian into his arms. And kissed her.

Miss Tibbles ought to have thought of the Winsboroughs. She ought to have cared what it might do to her reputation to be caught this way.

Instead she kissed him back. It was wrong, it was impossible, but she kissed him back. And the moment he let her go, she pulled free and, with tears obscuring her vision, fled the parlor and up to her room. There she shut and locked the door and leaned against it.

Horror filled Miss Tibbles' breast. The full enormity of what she had just done would not go away, no matter how many times she closed her eyes in an attempt to erase the image of Andrew's kiss and her response to it.

She was a governess! It had been her duty, for some

eighteen years, to suppress every such impulse in the girls she cared for. And now she had succumbed herself. How would she ever be able to present herself to a prospective employer and assure him or her that she could teach their daughter propriety when she had not mastered that lesson herself!

And yet, even as she chastised herself, a tiny image began to intrude, slowly growing larger. It was of herself, some twenty years ago. With Freddy Carrington. Remembering the first time he had kissed her. In the rose garden. It had been most improper, of course, but that had been half the attraction of doing so.

Oh, yes, Marian could remember that day all too clearly. And the days that followed. She had, it seemed, an impulsive nature, and a warm one. It was what made her so understanding of the girls placed in her charge, so able to outwit them. For she had been wild, once, herself.

But still! Eighteen years of ensuring that her nature did not once slip the leash of propriety only to have it happen here, in Bath! And before Annabelle and Lord Winsborough, of all people! If she thought Barbara's letter would be devastating, Marian did not want to even try to imagine what Annabelle might write to her sisters.

Even as she thought the girl's name, there was a soft rapping at the door. Marian wanted to pretend she was not there, but that would have been cowardly. She swung the door open and Annabelle slipped inside the room, eagerly.

"I came upstairs to tell you that you needn't worry, Miss Tibbles," Annabelle said, a trifle breathlessly. "I shan't tell anyone what we saw here today."

Marian was touched. "Thank you, my dear," she said, with some constraint.

They spoke for a few moments about other matters then Annabelle said, "I must go now. And, Miss Tibbles?"

"Yes, my dear?"

"I do hope you will marry the colonel. I want so very much for you to be happy and I think he would do his best to make you so."

Then, before Marian could remonstrate, Annabelle had slipped back out the door and was on her way downstairs. Which was, the governess thought wryly, entirely appropriate for how the day had already gone!

Chapter 7

Andrew stared after Marian's retreating back. It was not the first time he had kissed her, nor the first hint he had that she might possess a passionate nature. And yet this kiss had taken his breath away.

He wanted to follow her upstairs but he was far too conscious of the interested eyes of the Winsboroughs upon him and of how beyond the pale such a thing would be. No, he could not go after Marian. Instead he straightened his jacket, pasted a smile upon his face, and turned again to Lord Winsborough.

"So, tell me," he said, "what do you think of the latest news from the colonies."

As he had hoped, this provocation, deliberately intended to incense someone who had come from there, diverted Lord Winsborough's thoughts. A few minutes later, Lady Winsborough slipped out of the room. Gone to speak to Marian, no doubt. He only hoped she would not try to thrust a spoke in his wheels as so many seemed to wish to do.

At least Lady Winsborough, when she returned to the parlor to collect her husband, smiled warmly at him. She even wished him luck persuading Marian to marry him. It was an unusual but endearing gesture and Andrew was grateful for the kindness that prompted it.

Left alone in the parlor, he tried to decide whether he should send a message up to Marian or leave her alone for the rest of the day. What the devil had gotten into the woman anyway?

She was soft and sweet and well-bred. However much she might try to disparage herself in his eyes, she would never succeed. And yet at the same time, Colonel Merriweather was conscious of a certain sense of unease as well. She was a woman, a member of the fair but weaker sex. She ought to be deferring to him and to his opinions. Uneasily he began to wonder which was the real Miss Tibbles. Which was the woman he would be spending the rest of his life with, if he persuaded her to marry him. The gentle Marian, or the Marian who ripped up at him when her temper was crossed.

Eventually he decided against sending a message upstairs. No doubt Marian needed time alone. The experience of seeing his Aunt Cordelia must have been too unnerving and he was foolish to expect otherwise. He would go and find a flower shop and arrange for a posy of flowers to be sent. And he would try to make certain nothing overset her again any time soon.

Having thus thoroughly deluded himself as to the nature of his intended bride, Colonel Merriweather set off to put his plans into motion.

Upstairs Marian fingered the rich silk of her rose-colored gown hanging in the wardrobe. Was it so wrong for her to wish that she could wear such dresses every day? To wish that she could have frequent opportunities to wear them? To consider, just for a moment, the possibility of actually becoming Mrs. Merriweather?

She sighed. When had she become so missish? It was an image none of the girls she had taken care of, over the years, would have recognized. She had certainly had resolution enough on their behalf, so where had it gone when she needed some for herself?

Perhaps it was time to begin looking for another position after all. Reluctantly Miss Tibbles reached for her bonnet. She would need to go out and find a shop that sold the London papers. There she could see if anyone had advertised for a governess. Preferably as far away as possible from the county where Colonel Merriweather had his estate.

She did not think that even she would have the resolution to see him again once she took up another post as governess. Let him, she was female enough to wish, remember her like this, as a lady. Not as the drab sparrow she would be once she was again employed.

Downstairs the landlady, Mrs. Stonewell, eyed her oddly as she left the house, but said nothing. Marian grimaced. Would it always be like this? Living somewhere in between the status of a servant and someone on a par with the family? Firmly she pushed the thought out of her mind. The papers. She must purchase the papers.

She returned sometime later with several papers, not all of them from London. Resolutely she climbed the stairs to her room, resisting the urge to stop and gossip with some of the other ladies who were lodging there. In her room she went carefully through the advertisements, circling those that seemed promising. Then, before she could change her mind, she pulled out her writing materials and began to compose letters to the most select of these.

With luck she would have a post and be gone from Bath before Colonel Merriweather could realize what she intended to do and try to stop her. For she had no doubt he would try to stop her. Not that he could succeed, but Marian had no wish to engage in an argument with him when so large a part of her heart could only wish to lose.

No, best if he had no warning. And now she must hurry. There was little time to waste if she wished these letters to go out in the last post of the day.

*   *   *

At their country estate, Lord and Lady Westcott stared incredulously at Lady Farrington's letter, passing it back and forth between them.

"Miss Tibbles? Behaving scandalously in Bath?" Lady Westcott said with a bewildered air. "Surely it cannot be possible."

"A hum. All a hum. You'll see. Barbara cannot possibly mean what she seems to mean," the Earl of Westcott said, with great conviction.

"Are you certain?"

He cleared his throat nervously, but his voice was brisk as he replied, "Well, stands to reason, don't it? Think of the woman! Can you imagine her behaving improperly? I can't! And even if I could," he added as Lady Westcott started to protest, "can you imagine any gentleman wishing to have her behave improperly? Eh? Can you?"

Now that he put it that way, Lady Westcott had to admit that she could not. "I suppose it would be unlikely," she said. "Most men seem to prefer livelier creatures," she added diplomatically.

Westcott snorted. "Prettier creatures, you mean!" he retorted bluntly. "And Miss Tibbles ain't pretty. Don't mean to be unkind but no use wrapping it up in clean linen. She's plain."

Lady Westcott, who had more than once glimpsed Miss Tibbles without her glasses and with her hair hanging down her back, when she had to get up for one of the girls in the middle of the night, was not so certain. Still, she had to admit that her husband was a man and therefore more likely to be a proper judge of what a man would want to see in a woman. And what he would be likely to see—or not see—in Miss Tibbles.

Still, she wondered. Were it possible, she would have gone to Bath to see for herself. But it wasn't possible. They were expecting house guests within the week and one could not leave them to fend for themselves. No, she would just have to trust that Barbara had either mistaken what she thought she had seen or they were misreading what she had written. Which, considering the state of Barbara's penmanship, was not in the least unlikely, after all.

If only she could talk it over with her sister, Ariana. But Lady Brisbane was in London and not likely to come to what she disparagingly called the ends of the earth!

Lady Brisbane was pondering over some letters of her own. She had not received one from Barbara, but Cordelia, Lady Merriweather, had written. And in some agitation, too. Then there were one or two other letters that hinted Miss Tibbles had found something to entertain her in Bath.

It was all very odd. The image that came to mind, of a drab little creature, stern and intimidating, did not bear the slightest resemblance to anyone who could be called a temptress luring Cordelia's nephew to his doom with her feminine wiles. And yet that was precisely what Lady Merriweather accused Miss Tibbles of being and doing.

Worse, Cordelia seemed to think Ariana could and should do something about it. Well, they might be bosom bows, but Lady Brisbane was not about to hare off to Bath, just as arrangements had finally been made for her to take a trip to the Continent. No, indeed! Cordelia would have to deal with the matter herself.

Besides, it was all nonsense. Miss Tibbles was far too sensible a woman to allow her head to be turned by anyone, and far too old to turn any man's head herself. Cordelia was just a silly widgeon and by the time Ariana had returned, it would all turn out to have been a pack of nonsense.

Just in case, however, perhaps she should drop a word in a couple of ears that Miss Tibbles, that most wonderful of governesses, was again looking for a post. The Haldanes were known to be about to throw up their hands in despair over their two daughters. They would no doubt be delighted to hire Miss Tibbles.

And if that would not do, the Dalwimples were also looking for a new governess, the old one having fled the house in the middle of the night due to a mouse having been placed in her bed. Or the Thorntons. They needed Miss Tibbles, even if they didn't yet know it.

Hmmm, perhaps Ariana should not only speak to each of them in turn, but also drop a note to Miss Tibbles informing her of these possible opportunities. It would be as well to have her set up in a new post as soon as possible. It was all very well for her sister to pay for a holiday for the woman but really, if one were not careful, such extraordinary attention might well go to her head!

With a sigh of relief, having settled matters to her own satisfaction, Lady Brisbane set aside the letter from Lady Merriweather and turned instead to a gratifying pile of invitations from friends who wished to see her before she left on her trip.

And of course her niece, Penelope, with her husband, Mr. Talbot, was coming to dinner in a few days. She really ought to arrange something special with the cook for she was very fond of the pair.

In the north of England, another Westcott daughter, Rebecca stared at the letter in her hand. Around her, a group of noisy children were playing a game. Without once losing track of what they were doing, her husband, Hugh Rowland, managed to ask, "Is something wrong, my love?"

In answer, Rebecca handed him Barbara's letter. He read it, looked over at her, with one eyebrow cocked upward. "Is it possible?" he asked.

She gave him a withering look in reply.

"What do you wish to do?"

She tapped her chin thoughtfully. "I was wondering," she said slowly, taking the time to think through her answer, "whether there would be any way for you to find out anything about this Colonel Merriweather. Who he is, what he did in the military, what sort of man he might be."

He hesitated. "Ought we to interfere?" he asked.

Rebecca stared back gravely. "Miss Tibbles never hesitated to interfere, when it was for our best. Should I do less for her? If this Merriweather is some sort of mountebank, luring her into improper behavior, oughtn't we to find out? And warn her?"

Hugh sighed. He knew that look his lovely wife wore upon her face. He also remembered Miss Tibbles and could easily imagine what she might think of such interference. So again he tried to temporize.

"Miss Tibbles is a woman of excellent sense. I scarcely think it likely she would be taken in by a mountebank. Besides, the name Merriweather seems familiar. And in a positive way. Had there been some scandal, surely that would not be so."

Rebecca crossed her arms over her chest. Her expression became more mulish than ever. She began to tap her foot, not a good sign.

"I want you to check on Colonel Merriweather," she repeated.

Hugh sighed. He had been married long enough by now to know when an argument might be futile. "Very well," he said. "I shall write to some people I know in London. But mind, I want your promise you shall do nothing rash until we hear. If Miss Tibbles has found a gentleman who admires her, we have no right to cause her trouble."

"I won't," Rebecca fervently promised. "I should like to see her happy just as much as you would. I should never do anything that might jeopardize her happiness.

But you know a great many men, Bow Street Runners, do you not?" she asked. "Surely one of them could check into this Colonel Merriweather for us? And then I can be quite content to leave it to you to know what to do."

Reluctantly Hugh agreed. He only wished he could be certain it were true that Rebecca would leave matters in his hands. Not that she ever meant to cause problems, but he knew only too well that once Rebecca decided something needed to be done, she did it.

With a silent prayer sent heavenward, Hugh went off to write his letters. It went against the grain to hire a Bow Street Runner to look into the affairs of a fellow gentleman, and yet, considering his own involvement in an investigation of many fellow gentlemen, perhaps it was, after all, absurd to cavil at checking into one.

What could it hurt? If there was something to be found, it was right and proper to do so to protect Miss Tibbles. If there was not, why then he would be able to reassure both his wife and all her sisters. He did, indeed, know a good many Runners as a result of helping Sir Geoffrey Parker investigate a ring of thieves in London. Any one of them would do and he had to admit that he would feel better if he knew more about this Colonel Merriweather. The whole thing sounded so unlike the Miss Tibbles he knew!

With a trifle less reluctance than before, Hugh reached for his pen and paper.

Chapter 8

Miss Tibbles knew she ought to be strong enough to resist Colonel Merriweather's invitations to go to the theater and for walks and even to a ball. And most of the invitations she did manage to refuse.

But if he happened to encounter her, walking through the park, how could she send him to the roundabout without creating a public stir? And what could be considered scandalous about walking in such a public place?

But it felt scandalous. More so than if she had gone to the theater with him. For walking in the park argued a casual intimacy which should never have sprung up between them. As they walked, he seemed almost able to read her mind, to speak of things so very, very important to her. With every step, he was becoming more dear to her heart and that frightened Miss Tibbles.

If they happened to brush accidentally against one another it was as though a spark of fire heated her skin. Perhaps it wouldn't have been so difficult if Marian had been able to put the kisses out of her mind. But she could not. All she had to do was look at Merriweather to remember how it felt to have his lips pressing against hers, his body a hair's breadth away, his arms cradling her gently but firmly.

It was a great relief, therefore, when Marian received the first of the replies to her inquiries for a post and even an offer or two, unsolicited. One appointment had been arranged here in Bath, so that she need not travel all the way to London.

With a sigh, Marian pulled out the glasses she did not need and had not used since arriving here for her holiday. She also drew out of the wardrobe her plainest gown and pinned her hair into the most unbecoming style she could manage.

When she surveyed the results in the small looking glass in the room, Marian felt a distinct shock. She had not known how much it would hurt to go back to being that drab wren she had seemed for so many years. She had not counted on how much she would miss the freedom she had here in Bath to please herself. She had not guessed how bitterly she would resent hiding away all traces of any attractiveness that might make a man look at her twice.

Still, this was how it had to be. She stiffened her back, collected her reticule and bonnet, and the letter requesting her to call at York House at a certain hour and left her room without a backward look. Marian had become, once more, Miss Tibbles. She had not survived after her father's disgrace and death by repining over what could not be changed. She was not about to begin doing so now.

At the entrance to York House, Miss Tibbles paused. She drew in a breath and went inside, asking for the person named in the letter. Someone showed her up to a pleasant sitting room and asked her to wait.

She ought to have sat on the plainest chair, facing the door, hands folded primly in her lap. But she could not bring herself to do so. Instead, with one tiny, final act of rebellion, Miss Tibbles went to stand at the window, looking out at the street. She heard the door open and close behind her and only then did she turn around.

For an instant the room seemed to reel and she peered again at the letter she held in her hand, then at the young woman standing before her with an absurd grin upon her face, looking entirely unrepentant.

"You are not Mrs. Applewaite," Miss Tibbles said severely.

"Did I surprise you?" Diana, the Earl of Westcott's eldest daughter demanded.

"Very much so," Miss Tibbles retorted. "But where is Mrs. Applewaite? Or does she not even exist?"

Someone stepped around from behind Diana. It was a pleasant-looking, plump little woman, amiability written across her face. "I am Mrs. Applewaite," she said, coming forward to greet Miss Tibbles. "Lady Berenford and I are good friends and when she told me that you required a position, well, I could scarcely believe my good fortune. I have three daughters, you see, and I love them most dearly, but they are more than I can manage. Especially since I have been unable to find any governess who will remain above six months. Do you understand then, why I was so delighted, when Lady Berenford suggested your name to me?"

Miss Tibbles understood all right. She understood far too well. She understood right down to the tips of her toes. Here was a doting mother who could not bear to exercise the least discipline upon her daughters. And who no doubt could not bear to allow the governess to do so either.

Oh, yes, Miss Tibbles could picture only too well what her household must be like. Mrs. Applewaite would be a kind employer and her daughters absolute terrors. As always, Miss Tibbles would be expected to work her magic on the girls. And she could do it, too. Miss Tibbles had no doubts on that score. But the image filled her with misgivings. She was tired, so very tired, of living this kind of life.

Still, a woman in her position could not be choosy. At

least Mrs. Applewaite would be a kind employer. Indeed, her thoughts seemed to march in tune with Miss Tibbles.

"You shall be just like one of the family," Mrs. Applewaite promised. "Lady Berenford has told me something of your history and you need not fear that in my household anyone will treat you with anything less than the greatest respect and kindness."

Except the servants, who would resent her, Miss Tibbles thought bitterly. The more kindly she was treated by the family, the greater the resentment would be. Still, her lips formed the proper reply.

"You are very kind, Mrs. Applewaite. And if Lady Berenford recommends you, then I am sure I should be very fortunate to take up a post in your household."

Mrs. Applewaite beamed. "Good! Then it is all settled? You will come at the end of next week?"

Yes. She was supposed to say yes. Even as she tried to make herself speak that one simple word, the door to the sitting room was flung open and Colonel Merriweather stood there glowering at her.

But only for a moment. Then he stalked inside the room, not bothering to close the door behind him. Now there was a different expression on his face, one that seemed to hold anger and mischievous intent and compassion.

Fascinated, Mrs. Applewaite and Diana stared at Colonel Merriweather, and Miss Tibbles felt both relief and dismay at the sight of him. He moved with a sense of purpose but now that he was in the room he seemed to falter, as if he wasn't certain what to do next.

It was Diana who spoke first. She looked with lively interest from Miss Tibbles to Merriweather and seemed to see more than Marian would have liked.

"May we help you, sir?" Diana asked politely. "Perhaps you are in the wrong room?"

That seemed to recall Colonel Merriweather to his

manners. With poor grace he bowed and said, "Er, my apologies for bursting in on you like this. It is just that I, er, that is to say, I am Colonel Merriweather and I saw Miss Tibbles come in here and . . ."

His voice trailed off. Everyone stared at Merriweather waiting for more. Finally Marian could stand it no longer and she said, with some exasperation, "And what? Did you think I was here on an assignation? Well, I am not. And even if I were, it would be none of your affair!"

"But I would want it to be my affair!" he blurted out.

From Diana came a stifled burst of laughter. At Marian's quelling look, she struggled to put a dignified look upon her face and said, with creditable calm, "Miss Tibbles is here at my request. My friend, Mrs. Applewaite, is looking for a governess. They have settled that she will start at the end of next week."

The color seemed to drain from Colonel Merriweather's face. Marian reached out a hand toward him. She did not mean to do so. Indeed, she didn't even realize she had. Nor that she had taken a step toward him. Two steps, and then a third.

But she did hear herself say, "Colonel? Are you all right?"

He stared at her, pain patent in his deep gray eyes. "Why?" he whispered. "Is marriage to me so unbearable an alternative that you could not even give me a little more time to persuade you? Am I so wanting in character or charm or warmth that you would prefer the life of a governess, a servant, however superior, to that of being my wife? Do you truly hold me in such abhorrence?"

Shaken, Marian answered, her own face drained of color now, "No! Of course not! I have told you why I cannot marry you. Why you should not want me to do so. I am thinking of you!"

Bitterness etched lines into his face until Colonel Merriweather seemed to age ten years before their eyes.

"No," he said wearily. "If you cannot bear my company, that is one thing. But do not try to gammon me by saying you are refusing me for my own good."

Marian felt rather than saw Diana move to her side. Her whole attention was turned toward the Colonel. He was leaving. Which ought to be what she wanted. But there was such heaviness in his step, such defeat in his shoulders, that she could not bear it.

"Go after him!" Diana hissed.

Startled, Marian looked at the eldest Westcott daughter. Diana gave her a little push, and repeated her words. Miss Tibbles looked at Mrs. Applewaite, who was smiling at her sympathetically.

"Lady Berenford is quite right, you know," Mrs. Applewaite said cheerfully. "If you do not go after the colonel you will regret it for the rest of your life."

"But I cannot," Marian protested.

They both just looked at her and suddenly Miss Tibbles nodded decisively. She moved quickly to the doorway of the sitting room and was just in time to see Colonel Merriweather reach the foot of the stairs. Grabbing her skirts to keep from tripping, she hurried down after him.

He was already out the door by the time she reached the foot of the stairs, but Marian merely increased her speed. By the time she reached the street, she was all but running. Which she needed to do because Colonel Merriweather had increased his own stride.

Heedless of the spectacle she was making of herself, Marian began to run. She called out his name, retaining only a sufficient sense of propriety to keep it formal. "Colonel Merriweather!"

He stopped, turned slowly, as if afraid to believe his ears, and waited for her. It took Miss Tibbles only a moment more to reach him. There was dawning hope in his eyes, but still a wariness in his expression as he waited for her to speak.

He was waiting for her to say she was sorry and, perversely, Marian realized that she didn't in the least wish to do so. Instead she advanced upon him, with the most quelling look she had ever had to use on any of her charges. Then, without giving the colonel time to speak, she began her attack.

"How dare you intrude? How dare you presume to speak in such a way to me? And in front of others? If you think that I shall allow you to do so after we are married, you very much mistake the matter!"

His expression, which had gone from hopeful to incredulous to angry, now changed once more as he took in her words. His whole stance altered.

"After we are married?" he echoed, starting to advance upon her. "Does this mean we are going to be married?"

Marian found herself retreating. Still she did not give in. With a voice that fairly dripped of acid tones, she said, "If you are going to go about, creating scenes such as the appalling one I just witnessed, then I suppose I have no alternative other than to at least consider the notion. You have certainly not advanced my chances for acquiring a post as governess by that display."

He smiled at her. How dare Andrew smile at her like that? As if he could see past her sharp words clear down into her heart? As though he wanted to take her in his arms and keep her safe and protect her from ever having to face humiliation again?

Miss Tibbles sniffed. She distinctly sniffed. And he laughed. He leaned forward, kissed the tip of her nose, then pulled back and laughed again.

"I do not see what is so amusing," she said loftily. "I have only said that I will consider getting married."

"Of course," he said gravely even as he drew her arm through his.

Then he started walking and she had, perforce, to walk

with him unless she wished to create an even greater scene than she had already done.

"Once we are certain that we are going to be married," he said, "we shall have to set a date and inform our families and friends. We shall have to decide where we are going to be married and have the banns published there. I thought perhaps my estate? It would please my people to see us married there and you have said you have no real family left."

Miss Tibbles felt as if, with every step, she was sinking deeper and deeper into a morass. With each step he became more and more certain they would be married. He went from speaking of *if* to speaking of *when*. Finally, he talked as though the thing were as good as done.

It was folly! Wasn't it? Despite her moment of weakness it was impossible that she should marry him! Wasn't it? Miss Tibbles tried to recall the reasons she had told herself she could not marry the man. At the moment, she could remember none of them.

She looked up at him. He was glowing, positively glowing, as he talked of their future together. Plainly, it was useless to try to bring the man to his senses. Not when he was in a mood such as this! She would do so another day, when she could marshal her arguments more clearly.

It didn't occur to her that the colonel would be completely unable to keep the news to himself. Not once he had convinced himself it was as good as done. And even if it had, what, after all, could Marian have done?

Chapter 9

Marriage. It was, Miss Tibbles thought bitterly, a very final word. And one that engendered very strong emotions. She shuddered as she recalled Lady Merriweather shrieking, positively shrieking, "Married? No, no, a thousand times no! You cannot do this, Andrew!"

Or Diana hugging her and whispering how happy she was that her dear governess was getting married.

Or Mrs. Applewaite beaming approval, as though it was something in which she herself had had a hand.

Even her landlady, Mrs. Stonewell, seemed to have somehow heard the news and was beforehand offering her congratulations and wishes for Miss Tibbles' happiness.

Useless to try to convince anyone it was by no means a certain thing. Not when she could not convince herself it was not. Each time she opened her mouth to firmly deny the matter, an image of herself by his side, taking their wedding vows, made her close it again.

Miss Tibbles was not accustomed to being unable to make up her mind. It did not improve her mood. Nor did the fact that she could not decide whether the greater emotion she felt was anticipation or fear.

She was not in the best of moods, therefore, as she returned to her lodgings two mornings later, after a brisk walk, which she had taken alone, at an early hour, to try to clear her thoughts.

"Pssst."

Miss Tibbles paused and looked around. She saw no one. How odd.

"Pssst."

There it was again. Marian was not in the mood to be amused or scared or whatever it was she was supposed to feel at what was evidently a foolish prank.

"All right. Whoever you are, come out. Right this instant!" she commanded.

There was a brief silence, then a man slipped around from the corner of the building where he had been hiding.

He was a rough-looking individual and for a moment Miss Tibbles had the sense to be afraid. Then she looked closer and pegged him for precisely who he was.

"You are a Bow Street Runner," she said severely.

For a moment he looked chagrined. Then, with an admiring note to his voice he agreed.

"You've caught me out, all right and tight. Fairly bowled over I am that you did so quick."

"Yes, well, I should be greatly obliged if you would tell me what you mean by behaving in such an absurd manner!" Miss Tibbles told him roundly.

He rubbed his scruffy chin. "Well, it's like this, you see. I be looking for a Miss Tibbles."

Marian stared at him incredulously. "For me? Why on earth should you do so?"

He looked around to make certain there was no one nearby before he leaned closer to her and said, with a wink, "I was told to come and give you me report. And give it only to you. Ain't no colonels hanging about, are there?"

Now Marian truly lost her temper. "Do you see any colonels lurking about?" she demanded. "There are no bushes to hide behind and you were at the corner of the street! Or perhaps you suspect him of following me along the rooftops? Or running into doorways so as to play least in sight?"

"Here now! There's no reason to come over me so heavy-handed!" the Runner protested. "I'm only doing as I were told."

Marian crossed her arms over her chest and began to tap her foot impatiently. Any of her former pupils would have known to run as far and as fast as possible away from her. But the poor Runner, it seemed, had no choice but to stay and listen to Miss Tibbles.

"Who told you to come and speak to me?" she asked skeptically.

"Well, strictly speaking, it were the fellow what hands out our assignments . . ." He paused, took one look at Miss Tibbles' face, and hastily added, "Of course what you really means is what bloke paid for me services. A Mr. Rowland, I believes."

"Hugh?" Marian gasped in disbelief.

"They didn't tell me the mort's given name," the Runner grumbled.

"Yes, well, never mind," Miss Tibbles said impatiently. "Just tell me what this report is that you are supposed to deliver."

The Runner promptly pulled his notebook out of his coat pocket and began to read. "Subject. A bloke what calls himself Colonel Merriweather, given name Andrew. Nephew to Lady Merriweather, younger brother of current Lord Merriweather. Served in His Majesty's forces, for some twenty-two or twenty-three years. Sold out a few months ago after he inherited a tidy estate from his dead wife."

"And why are you telling me all this?" Marian asked, more impatient than ever.

"I told you," the Runner said, as though speaking to someone severely wanting in wits, "I was paid to do it.

Now, where was I? Right, this Colonel Merriweather has an income of some eight thousand pounds a year. The estate is unencumbered. So is the colonel. He is not now married, though he was. His wife died a year ago in what you might call suspicious circumstances. Very suspicious indeed, considering she died right after she inherited an estate. The estate what's now his. The colonel, he weren't never brought to trial but there are those as says he ought to of been."

The Runner snapped his notebook shut and stared at Miss Tibbles with some concern. "That's all I has. So far," he said.

"So far?" Marian echoed.

He nodded. "Don't you worry none. I'll find things out. Like a ferret I am. And as the colonel is here in Bath, I'll stay in Bath as well and find out what I can about what he's up to now."

This could not be happening, Marian thought, but of course it was. From the determined look on the Runner's face, no amount of argument would have persuaded him to abandon his assignment.

He stared at her expectantly and with a tiny sigh Marian opened her reticule and drew out a coin to give him. He took it gratefully.

"Thank you, ma'am. You won'ts regret it. A proper job I'll do, I will."

"I'm certain you will," Marian said faintly, thinking that perhaps she ought to warn Andrew about the Runner.

His next words stopped her. "I aims to give value, I does. So here's something at no charge. He knows about your nest egg, he does. The one what you ain't never made no move to claim."

Two thoughts ran through Marian's mind. She asked the second one first. "I have a nest egg?"

"Aye, left you by your aunt. With a solicitor in London. I has the address, if you wants it."

She nodded and listened as he gave it to her. "My Aunt Sophia," she murmured to herself. "It must have been my Aunt Sophia."

"Aye, that's the name," the Runner agreed.

"But how do you know about it?" Miss Tibbles demanded. "And what did you mean when you said that 'he' did. Do you mean Colonel Merriweather? How could he?"

"Aye, that's exactly who I mean," the Runner said, nodding his head vigorously. "Hired one of me comrades, he did, to find out all about you. Me friend found out about the nest egg. And when he heard what I was hired to do, he told me all about it."

Dazed, Marian made herself ask, "Do you know how much the nest egg might be?"

The Runner smiled smugly. He named a figure which, while it would certainly not make Miss Tibbles rich, did mean that if she chose, she need not ever be a governess again. If she were willing to live quietly in some remote hamlet far from the expense of fashionable watering holes or cities.

The Runner leaned close. "You ain't about to faint on me, is you?" he asked suspiciously.

That recalled Marian to herself. She stared at him and said, haughtily, "I never faint."

"In course you don't," he agreed, as though humoring her. "But mayhaps you oughts to step around to your lodgings and take a lie down anyways. Just as a precaution like, you might say."

That was, Marian had to agree, a suggestion which perhaps had considerable merit. This had, after all, been an astonishing conversation and she now had a great deal to think over.

And besides, she had a letter to write to a solicitor in London! If this news were true, it altered a great many things. If it were also true that Andrew—Colonel Merriweather—had investigated her, it altered a great many more.

As though he were following her thoughts by the expressions that chased themselves across her face, the Runner abruptly told Miss Tibbles, "Don't forget now about his first wife. It were a very shady death. Meself, I would have arrested him and tried him for murder. But I guess they does things differently in France."

And that was the final straw. Miss Tibbles drew herself up straight and said, crisply, "I shall think about everything you have told me. Good day."

"Good day to you, ma'am. If you can have a good day after what I've just told you," he added gloomily.

To her great relief, however, he looked around, then briskly set off in a direction opposite to that of her lodgings. Marian did not want to have to try to explain such an odd-looking creature to the landlady. Her circumstances there had drawn quite enough attention already and she did not wish for any more!

She was also relieved to find there were no notes, no messages, no little presents today from Colonel Merriweather when she reached her lodgings.

The landlady misunderstood her concern and said soothingly, "Never you mind, Miss Tibbles. I'm certain your gentleman will send something around later. That's if he don't come himself. Which I'm quite certain he will, as often as he likes to pop by to see you."

With a frisson of fear, Marian realized Mrs. Stonewell was right. Colonel Merriweather would most probably come by. She felt a sense of panic as she realized she was not ready to see him. Not just yet. She needed time to think over what the Runner had told her and she needed to post some letters, one to the solicitor and another to Rebecca and Hugh. Though whether she meant to thank them or to send them a blistering scold she hadn't quite decided yet.

"Are you all right, Miss Tibbles?" Mrs. Stonewell asked, with some concern.

Marian seized upon the question gratefully. "No. No, I am not. I think I had best go upstairs and lie down."

"You do that," the landlady said soothingly. "I'll have some nice hot tea and soup sent up for you."

"Yes, and if Colonel Merriweather comes, would you tell him I am very sorry but I am not able to see him today?" Marian persisted.

"Of course I will," Mrs. Stonewell assured her. "And most anxious I'll be bound he'll be. But don't you fret. I run a respectable house. He'll not be allowed above stairs. He'll just have to wait until you feel well enough to receive him. And you will, soon enough. A day or two to settle your stomach and you'll be right as a trivet, I've no doubt."

"Thank you," Miss Tibbles said warmly.

With a strong sense of relief she mounted the stairs, blissfully unaware that the landlady planned to send around a note to Colonel Merriweather immediately informing him that his lady love was feeling poorly. Had she known, Marian might well have been tempted to pack her bags and flee Bath at once.

Or at the very least, this boardinghouse!

Upstairs, turning over in her mind what the Runner had told her, Marian had to admit to some trepidation. And yet she could not help remembering that there had been a time when it looked as if Winsborough had had a hand in murdering his cousin for his estate. But he had not. And perhaps the rumors were just as false regarding Andrew and his first wife.

No matter how she tried, she could not imagine him hurting anyone. And yet, neither could she imagine him hiring a Bow Street Runner to investigate her. Clearly there was a great deal she did not know about the man!

Indeed, if one were talking about appearances, how could she be certain the Bow Street Runner was who he claimed to be? Or that Rebecca and Hugh had hired him, as he said? And how was she to know whether anything he told her about Colonel Merriweather's supposed interest in her supposed inheritance was true?

Marian reached for her writing desk. She would write Rebecca and ask about the Runner. As for the solicitor, perhaps instead of writing to him directly, she should ask someone to approach him on her behalf. Someone who could see if he was the genuine article or whether some part of an elaborate scheme. After all, the address she had came from the supposed Runner.

But who could she ask? The Westcotts had returned to their country estate and even Miss Tibbles hesitated to ask Lady Brisbane to do her such a favor. Then she remembered. Another Westcott daughter, Penelope, and her husband, Mr. Talbot, were still in London. At least she thought they were. Perhaps they would be willing to visit the solicitor on her behalf and try to discover the truth of the matter. Then, if the legacy did turn out to be real, Marian could make the journey to London herself and claim her inheritance.

The letters were written with typical efficiency and soon ready to be sent out. True to her word, the landlady brought up tea and a nourishing broth.

Unfortunately, she also brought up a posy of flowers. From Andrew. And a book of poems. From Andrew. And a fan, from Andrew.

She ought to call him Colonel Merriweather. It was only right and proper to do so. But looking at the presents spread out on the bed, chosen with such care for her tastes, Marian could not. In her heart, no matter what he had done, he was Andrew.

Still, the presents made her uneasy. They did not arrive all at once, of course. No, the presents arrived over the course of the afternoon, leaving Marian more bewildered than ever as to why he was sending them. And full of guilt. She was, after all, deceiving him.

And yet, what else could she do? If Andrew saw her, he would read at once from her face something of what she had learned. And she would not be able to resist warning him about the Runner.

It was not, precisely, that Miss Tibbles was suspicious by nature. But eighteen years as a governess had taught her that one had to be wary. That the kindest face could hide a cruel heart. And if ever she had need to keep her wits about her, it was now.

Andrew was very confused. Entirely bewildered, in fact. The landlady at Miss Tibbles' lodgings seemed to think his offerings would be most acceptable to Marian, but she had yet to acknowledge any of them.

Perhaps she really was feeling very poorly, but according to the landlady it was nothing serious. And if it wasn't serious, then why hadn't she dashed off a brief note to thank him for his presents and to tell him how she was doing? It really was unlike her to be so inconsiderate. At least he thought it was.

The other odd thing was that he thought, from time to time, he caught a glimpse of someone following him about. Dashed pickpockets! They were becoming almost as common here as they were said to be in London. Still, he spared only a few moments on the fellow. His thoughts were primarily concerned with the state of Marian's health.

Perhaps it was the strain of all the interest shown by their acquaintances, he decided. If that should prove to be the case, then perhaps he should hire a carriage and, on the next fine day, take her for a drive in the hills outside of Bath. The sunshine and fresh air would do her good and they could enjoy the sort of privacy that was all but impossible here within the confines of the town proper.

Rather pleased with himself, Colonel Merriweather set off to make the necessary arrangements. Then he returned to Miss Tibbles' lodgings and the sympathy of her very kind landlady who, it seemed, enjoyed nothing better than a touch of romance and was eager to help further his suit.

Chapter 10

By the next morning, Miss Tibbles was herself again. To be sure, the things the Bow Street Runner had told her were shocking but she had a notion or two of her own. She was not a woman generally given over to the megrims. Instead she decided to take action for herself.

It would take time for her to hear back from the Talbots. Or from Rebecca and Hugh. Meanwhile, she could write to others she knew. And Miss Tibbles knew quite a few people. Among them were the families she had worked for, over the years. She had, after all, kept in touch with most of the girls even after they married.

A discreet letter asking if any one of them knew of a Colonel Merriweather might bring information. Information that not even a Bow Street Runner would be likely to be able to discover.

The world of the *ton* was an insular one. Families knew families and someone would be bound to know things that were supposed to be secrets, things that were whispered about, but only among one's own circle. Someone would be bound to be able to tell dear old Miss Tibbles something.

Marian was counting on it. Meanwhile, although it was tempting to continue to hide in her room, she could not do so forever. Nor was she truly inclined to continue such behavior. She had never been a coward and she did not intend to become one now.

Besides, Andrew was not likely to soon become discouraged. It made far more sense, therefore, to go down and see him when he came to call. She was curious to see if he would seem different, now that she looked at him through eyes made wary by what the Bow Street Runner had told her.

Marian dressed with care. She prided herself on her ability to judge character. What need, then, did she have to be afraid of Andrew? If he were not what he seemed, she would know it.

Or so she told herself. And yet there was a part of her which didn't want to question him, didn't want to look for flaws. Realizing this, Miss Tibbles shook herself impatiently. She would not tolerate such nonsense! Not in her charges, not in herself.

With a curt nod to the mirror, Marian went downstairs to greet Colonel Merriweather when Mrs. Stonewell came to tell her he was waiting to see her.

He rose to his feet instantly, at the sight of her. And what some might have called a besotted smile appeared on his face. In spite of herself, Marian felt her resolve falter. How could she suspect this man of anything nefarious? She asked herself.

Very easily, a little voice whispered in her head, reminding her of other villains she had known who had looked to be charming as well.

Still, she smiled and held out her hands to him. "Colonel Merriweather! How kind of you to come and see me. And to send such lovely presents yesterday."

He tried to draw her closer, but stopped the moment he felt her resistance. His voice was warm, as though with suppressed emotion, as he said, "Not nearly as lovely as you, my dear! No, don't turn your head away. I know you do not care for compliments, but I mean what I say."

Then, when she could not gather the words to reply, he went on, gently, "Do you feel well enough to go for a walk with me? It is a cool, sunny day and I cannot help but feel the fresh air would do you good. You are still looking a trifle peaked, you know."

That made Marian laugh, as perhaps it was meant to. "You are less than flattering to notice, sir!" she said. "But kind. And yes, I should like to go for a walk with you. My indisposition was a short-lived one."

He grinned. The man actually grinned! If he was acting, he was remarkably clever at it. Miss Tibbles shook herself. She could not, must not, let doubt overwhelm her. What if Colonel Merriweather were just what he seemed? She would be throwing away every chance for happiness by regarding him with constant suspicion.

And yet, Marian could not entirely let down her guard. As they walked, leisurely, toward the public gardens, she tried to delicately discover what she could.

"Do you know, Colonel Merriweather, you have told me very little of your last few years in the military, except to say that you were with Wellington in Paris, as part of the occupation," she said as lightly as she could. "You have told me a great deal of the early days but I am curious about more recent times as well."

He laughed self-consciously. Was there an edge to it? Then he said, avoiding her eyes, "Well, I saw far more of the action in the early years, you know. Recent times had me more likely to be dancing attendance on political visitors. Or writing reports. Very quiet, these past few years have been, for me."

"Except for Waterloo, surely?" she protested."

"Except for Waterloo," he gravely agreed.

Miss Tibbles felt a hint of frustration. Still, she was not daunted. She pressed on.

"And were you never lonely?" she asked.

"Lonely? Surrounded by so many other officers?" he seemed surprised by the question.

She let herself lean a little toward him. "Yes, but

didn't you miss the chance for female companionship? Didn't you wish for a wife?"

He went very still and did not answer. Then Marian said the most outrageous thing she could think of, something which could, with anyone else, put her beyond the pale. She asked, daringly, "Or did you have a mistress?"

He could have laughed and shrugged it off. He could have said she ought not to talk of such things. Instead, Colonel Merriweather was silent far too long. As though her shot had hit home.

And when Andrew did finally try to reply, there was a forced note to his voice, though he tried very hard to sound at ease.

"You shock me, Miss Tibbles! What do you know of mistresses?" he asked with an artificial heartiness in his voice, trying to turn her question aside.

In for a penny, in for a pound. She had already been outrageous, why not a little more? Perhaps then he would tell her what she wished to know.

"Ah, so you did have one?" she chided him, as if playfully roasting a friend.

Again there was silence. Then, quietly, soberly, "No. No, I did not."

Another silence, for Marian could think of no way to ask more bluntly about his supposed wife. But in the end she did not need to ask. He told her anyway.

"I had a wife. I suppose that sooner or later you will hear of her. She died just over a year ago," Merriweather said, the constraint evident in his voice. "We were married, Drusilla and I, for some eight years, though it was only after Waterloo that she was able to come and stay with me, where I was posted."

There was no need to pretend sympathy, Marian felt it instinctively for him. "I am so sorry!" Then, because she could not help herself, she asked, "Do you still miss her terribly?"

"Every day," was the sober reply.

Marian did not doubt him. Every line of his body, every line of his face, every note of agony in his voice bespoke the grief Andrew still felt. Was it possible he had killed his wife in a fit of anger and then regretted such a deed? She didn't know.

She must have made some sort of sound for now he looked at her and he said, "I will not, I cannot talk about Drusilla except to say that she was not a happy woman and now at least her suffering is over."

And what was there to say to that? Miss Tibbles devoutly hoped her face did not express the shock she felt, but there was very little she could do to command her emotions. Perhaps he would not notice.

But he did. He lifted her gloved hand and kissed the back of it. "Please, Marian, you must not be distressed," Andrew said, "or I shall regret telling you anything. You were meant to be happy and I shall do everything in my power to ensure that you are. So please, I pray you, don't grieve for Drusilla."

She could not bring herself to reprove him for using her name so familiarly. After all, he believed they were to be married. She forced herself to smile. It was a horrid smile, but the best she could do.

She also forced herself to say, brightly, "Well, now I understand why you do not wish to speak of the past few years. I have only myself to blame for asking."

As though entering into the spirit of the game, Colonel Merriweather wagged a finger at her and said, playfully, "There, you see my dear? That's what comes of excessive curiosity. You'd best not pry too closely into my affairs or heaven only knows what secrets of mine you may find that you do not like."

Now it was Marian who dared not meet his eyes! How could he jest about such a matter? Surely it meant he must be innocent of the charges? Or was he so certain he had escaped detection, escaped punishment, that he dared be as brazen as he wished?

Whatever was she to do?

Fortunately, the man seemed to take her response for natural confusion and he became more gentle than ever. Andrew even insisted on buying her some flowers from a girl selling posies. And he talked of some of the latest gossip of the town.

Marian was grateful for the time to compose herself. And she tried to forget that she might be walking in the gardens with a murderer. Perhaps that was why she did not notice the Bow Street Runner following them.

James Wilkerson was most upset to see the lady walking again with the colonel. It worried him, it did. What were she thinking? He'd told her what he knew. Any sensible lady ought to of known to stay away from the gent.

Mind you, he hadn't found anything certain. Yet. But he wouldn't have wanted his sister walking out with a gent what had so many suspicions against him, he wouldn't. Maybe he'd best speak to her again, when she were alone. He were being paid to protect her, he were, as well as to find out about the gent.

But how he could protect her if she insisted on doing such fool things was beyond him, and so he would write to the gent what was paying him straight away. He were due to send off a report by the end of the week anyway. He'd try to speak to the lady before then and maybe he'd be able to make her see reason. If not, he'd have to keep a closer watch than he already was keeping. And that didn't sit well with James Wilkerson. That didn't sit well at all.

Chapter 11

Penelope stared at the letter in her hand. Soot smudged the edges for she had not stopped to wash her hands of the results of the latest experiment she and Mr. Talbot were performing before opening the letter from Miss Tibbles.

A sharp exclamation brought Geoffrey to her side. "What is it, my love?" he asked.

"Miss Tibbles!" Penelope said, in a wondering tone of voice.

"Ah, yes. Didn't your sister write that she was behaving oddly? Is this more of the same?" Geoffrey asked. "And weren't we going to go to Bath next week to see what it was all about?"

Penelope looked up at him, a trifle unsteadily. "Well, yes and no. Barbara did write and so did Annabelle and Diana and we did plan to go next week. But this is something even more extraordinary. Miss Tibbles herself writes to ask if we will undertake a commission for her."

"What sort of commission?" Geoffrey asked, most sensibly, his attention as much on the page of the book he was perusing as on the conversation with his wife.

Penelope reached out and placed her hand across the page. "Geoffrey, listen to me! This is important," she said.

He sighed and gave up his efforts to focus on the book. When she was certain she had his full attention, Penelope went on, "Miss Tibbles asks that we visit a solicitor on her behalf and discover if there is an inheritance waiting for her. If so, she wishes to know how much it might be. And whether this solicitor is to be relied upon."

"I suppose you want to do this as soon as possible?" he asked.

She nodded and he glanced at the clock over the mantel. "Well," he said with a mock sigh, "I suppose you will be unable to focus on the experiment until we have looked into this matter for Miss Tibbles? Very well. If we hurry, we may still go this afternoon."

In answer, Penelope threw her arms around Geoffrey, requiring that a basin of clean water and clean clothes be called for before they could leave the house.

Eventually, however, all traces of the experiment were eradicated from their persons, the staff had managed to persuade them to take a bit of nourishment, and they were finally ready to set out.

Penelope carried the letter in her hand rather than in her reticule so that she could consult the address. At least she did so until Geoffrey gently took it from her and read off the address of the solicitor to the coachman.

Somewhat to her surprise, the fellow turned out to have offices in a very respectable part of town. And a large, clean office with a respectably sized staff. Clearly he was well established and accustomed to dealing with Quality, for his staff knew to show Mr. and Mrs. Talbot into an elegantly appointed waiting room, quite unlike the benches in the outer office where one or two other, less well-to-do clients waited their turn.

And when they were shown into the solicitor's presence, he was all deference. He did express some surprise that Miss Tibbles had not come herself.

"Indeed," he said, polishing his glasses, "I am very glad you have come on her behalf. I and my staff had not been able to locate her. Her family appeared to have lost track of her and she was not to be found at any lodgings for genteel ladies that we tried."

"Miss Tibbles has been a governess since soon after her father's death," Penelope said.

"A governess! Bless my soul! No one told me that!" the solicitor said, blinking rapidly.

"The inheritance?" Geoffrey said, trying to bring him back to the point at hand.

"Yes, yes, of course. Indeed. If Miss Tibbles has been a governess then of course she will wish to know of an inheritance that would allow her to cease to pursue such an onerous occupation. Mind you, it will not allow her to live an extravagant life, but if she has been a governess she will not be accustomed to one anyway."

It began to grate on Penelope's nerves that the solicitor should so disparage something Miss Tibbles had done so well, for so many years.

"Miss Tibbles was a superb governess," Penelope said through gritted teeth.

"Yes, yes, I've no doubt she was," the solicitor said hastily. With a very thin smile he said, "I certainly meant no disrespect. It is just that very few of my clients are, er, in service."

"What a pity," Penelope said sweetly, ignoring Geoffrey's warning look. "You have missed out on a great deal if you have never known anyone like Miss Tibbles."

He cast her an odd glance, then looked at Geoffrey, who merely shrugged. The solicitor appeared to decide that this was one of those situations where one ought to ignore such eccentricities.

One did not, after all, offend those who carried the aura of gentility and money about them as the Talbots did. He therefore did not reply to Penelope's sally but merely picked up the papers before him and read a moment, as though to refresh his memory. Then he removed his spectacles and folded his hands on the desk. He explained, briefly but to the point, the details of the inheritance. Then he had a question of his own.

"Can you tell me," he said, "when Miss Tibbles is likely to come to London to claim her inheritance herself? It would be possible, of course, to make arrangements to have funds sent to her, for her expenses in coming, if that should be a problem. But certain documents really must be signed by her, in person."

"And of course you could not possibly go to Bath to call upon her," Penelope said, sarcastically. "Miss Tibbles is not important enough for you to do so, is she? Particularly now that you know she has been a governess."

Now the solicitor looked distinctly affronted. In alarm Geoffrey said, heartily, "Of course not, my dear! You are roasting him and he does not know it. Miss Tibbles would not expect him to come to Bath on her behalf but she would expect you to deal with him with respect."

With that warning to remind her, Penelope managed a small apology, though her expression was still a trifle mutinous. Then, rising to her feet she said, "We shall of course write to Miss Tibbles at once with the news. I am certain you will hear from her directly very soon."

The solicitor rose as well. He frowned and said, thoughtfully, "May I ask how Miss Tibbles came to hear about her inheritance?"

Penelope and Geoffrey looked at one another. She pulled out the letter yet once again and perused it but it did not say. She would have shown it to the solicitor but guessed he might not like the distrust of him that Miss Tibbles had expressed.

Instead Penelope said, with a slight frown of her own, "Why, we do not know how she came to hear of her inheritance. She does not say in her letter."

He nodded. "I only ask because one other gentleman came to ask about the inheritance before you. In fact, I was somewhat surprised to hear how little you seemed to know and therefore, by extension, Miss Tibbles. He promised to acquaint her, you see, with all the details and I was curious if he had indeed finally done so."

"And who was this gentleman?" Geoffrey asked.

"A Colonel Merriweather," was the succinct reply.

Penelope and Geoffrey looked at one another in alarm.

"Did he say why he came to you? Or how he had heard of the inheritance?" Penelope asked carefully.

"Now that you mention it, he did not," the solicitor replied. "How odd. I had the impression, of course, that Miss Tibbles had asked him to look into her affairs and that she had told him about it. I did not like to ask why she had not come forward before, if she knew. After all, the legacy has been waiting for her for some eight years."

Penelope blinked. "Eight years?"

The words were scarcely a whisper. If Miss Tibbles had known, eight years ago, that there was such a legacy waiting for her, would she ever have become the Westcott governess? It was a thought which brought a profound sense of loss. Penelope could not imagine how her life would have turned out had Miss Tibbles not come into it. She did not wish to imagine such a thing. Nor did her husband, Mr. Talbot.

The solicitor looked from one to the other. "Is there some difficulty? Some problem?" he asked anxiously. "Was I indiscreet in speaking so frankly to this Colonel Merriweather? Or to you about him? He seemed to have formed a deep attachment to Miss Tibbles."

"Before or after he learned of her inheritance?" Geoffrey asked grimly.

"Oh, now, I hardly think her inheritance is sufficiently large to tempt a man of his circumstances!" the solicitor protested.

"And what, precisely, are his circumstances?" Geoffrey asked tightly.

"Why, I don't precisely know," the solicitor admitted.

"I merely meant that he looked like a man of means. And he did say he was related to Lady Merriweather so I presumed he was quite well-to-do."

Again Penelope and Geoffrey looked at one another. "Come," he said to her. "Let us go and see if anyone can tell us more about Lady Merriweather's nephew."

"Aunt Ariana, Lady Brisbane, knows Lady Merriweather well," Penelope said thoughtfully. "Perhaps she can tell us more."

"Excellent notion!" Geoffrey said heartily. "Let us go and call upon her at once."

The solicitor could only be said to be relieved to see them both go. Indeed, as they left, Penelope was conscious that the solicitor was mopping his brow. It served him right, she thought savagely. How dare he take such an attitude toward her dear Miss Tibbles?

Back in Bath, Colonel Merriweather had no notion he was the object of such curiosity. Or that anyone else was aware of Marian's inheritance.

Instead, he devoted himself to enjoying her company. Whatever her indisposition, days earlier, she seemed to have recovered completely and to be happy to spend time in his company, though her questions were occasionally a trifle strange and she held him at a bit of a distance.

But that was all right. She was, despite her years as a governess, a lady. She ought to hold him at a distance. Andrew was not in the least dismayed. Indeed, he felt about as content as a man could feel. After Drusilla's death he'd thought he would never, could never, feel this way about a woman again. It was very nice to know he'd been wrong.

He didn't question how or why Marian had come into his path, he was only very grateful she had. He was grateful to walk with her in the gardens. He was grateful for the times she looked at him in a way that made him want to draw her into his arms and make love to her, right then and there, and to the devil with anyone who might be watching.

But he could not treat Marian so. He cared far too much for her happiness and well-being. She was the one who would suffer from the sting of venomous tongues. Why, look at what had happened when he had forgotten himself before and one of her former charges had seen them!

So Andrew kept his wishes in check and merely walked, the picture of propriety, with Marian at his side, her hand tucked into the corner of his elbow.

He regretted that she had asked about his wife. He regretted that he had had to tell her about Drusilla. But he had known the question must come up, sooner or later. And he thought he had brushed through that ordeal tolerably well. There was no doubt he had shocked her, but with luck she would not think to look beyond what he had said and ask more pointed questions about how Drusilla had died.

Questions Andrew had no intention of answering. Ever, if he could help it. No, he was not going to risk having anyone find out what had happened to his wife.

He'd gone stiff as he thought of Drusilla and now Miss Tibbles was looking at him with a quizzical expression in her eyes. He forced himself to relax and turn her attention to a particularly riveting piece of gossip he had heard the night before.

It was very diverting, he thought, watching the warring halves of her expression. The prim and proper governess had been well trained to repress gossip by her charges and such habits die hard. And yet the other part of her, the woman, was as fascinated as anyone to hear the latest foolishness committed by the Prince of Wales.

And then he managed to turn the talk to her. And the families she had worked for. She would not speak any ill

of them, she had too much integrity for that, his Marian
did. But she told him little stories that made him laugh.
And for that he was grateful.

Sometimes he thought that was what he liked best
about Miss Tibbles. Her ability to make him laugh, to
make him feel at peace with himself. He had not felt that
way in a long time.

He knew she did not understand why he had chosen
her when he might have looked much higher. He could
have told her, of course, that the circumstances surround-
ing Drusilla's death had been more than enough to cause
mothers to want to keep their daughters from him. In
other circumstances, he might have jested that it was her
inheritance which had attracted him.

But she didn't know, yet, about the inheritance.

There were a lot of things Marian didn't know about
and, for the moment, Andrew intended to keep it that
way.

Marian stared up at Colonel Merriweather and wondered at the odd expression on his face. She still did not
feel altogether comfortable in his company, but neither
could she bring herself to refuse to see him. The only
thing she had done was to tell him, quite plainly and
firmly, that he must not yet presume the wedding to be
definite.

He had smiled and nodded and patted her hand and
looked at her in that infuriating way that men have when
they are certain they know better than the woman they are
with. At least he did not press her for a reason, chalking
it up to the propensity of women to vacillate. It was not
an image of herself that Miss Tibbles could contemplate
with any great degree of composure, but it was better
than having to tell him what the Bow Street Runner had
told her.

Impatiently Marian wondered how soon she could

begin to receive replies to the letters she had written. She wondered how soon Penelope would write to tell her the truth about her supposed inheritance.

And most of all, she wondered when she would be able to know whether to trust her head or her heart.

Chapter 12

Marian had scarcely finished dressing and pinning up her hair, two days later, when the landlady rapped smartly on her door.

"There is a"—Mrs. Stonewell sniffed—"person, a Mr. Wilkerson, downstairs who insists on speaking with you! I hope you do not have creditors pursuing you?"

"No, no, I am certain I do not," Miss Tibbles said hastily.

"Then I may send him away with a flea in his ear?" the landlady asked, hopefully.

Marian would have liked to agree, but she had a horrible feeling she knew who it was. And if she did not see him here, he was likely to follow her about on the street. So, with a sigh she shook her head.

"No, I shall come down and see who it is. Then I may send him away with a flea in his ear!"

That, at any rate, appeared to satisfy the landlady.

Downstairs, Marian discovered that her fears were indeed correct. It was the Bow Street Runner.

"What on earth are you doing here?" she demanded, with pardonable exasperation.

"I needs to see you," he said. "And there weren't no chance without the colonel was about."

Miss Tibbles began to tap her foot, only too conscious of the landlady nearby, no doubt with her ear pressed against the door.

"This is not a good place either," she retorted. Lowering her voice, she added, "The landlady is likely to tell the colonel you were here."

"The devil!"

"Precisely." She relented a trifle at the appalled look on his face and added soothingly, "Mind you, she assumes you are a bill collector. I told her otherwise but I could see she did not believe me."

"Yes, well, I won'ts come calling here again, then. I just thought I oughts to see you. And give you this. Here," he said, pulling a sheaf of papers out of his pocket and shoving them at her, "I was going to send these to Mr. Rowland. But you takes and reads them. I'll writes out another set for him."

Reluctantly, Marian took the papers the Runner held out to her. She didn't really want to look at them, but it was the only way she could think of to persuade the man to go. Besides, a little voice hinted in her ear, it wouldn't hurt to see what he had written about Colonel Merriweather. It wouldn't hurt to know what was being said. Perhaps these pages would even clear Andrew, though that scarcely seemed likely given the urgency with which the man pressed them on her and the way he spoke.

The Runner began to back toward the door. "Don't worrit none," he said. "I'll still be out and about watching over you."

Then, before she could tell him she didn't wish him to do so, the Runner pulled open the door, nearly spilling the landlady into the room. The Runner edged past Mrs. Stonewell and Marian tried to hide the sheaf of papers behind her, though it was evident from the look on the woman's face that she didn't succeed.

The landlady had such a grim look that Miss Tibbles started toward the stairs to her room, only too well aware that Mrs. Stonewell hadn't even tried to justify listening at the parlor door.

But then, with the care Marian had taken, she didn't think that Mrs. Stonewell could really have overheard anything of importance. Which no doubt helped to account for the woman's bad mood.

"My dear Miss Tibbles," Mrs. Stonewell said, with patently false sweetness, "while my lodgers are certainly allowed to have callers, I expect them not to abuse the privilege. An occasional use of the parlor is to be expected but I pray you will understand when I say that to be commandeering it as often as you have, of late, is rather beyond the line of what is pleasing."

As the landlady was still trying to get a glimpse of the sheaf of papers she held behind her, Marian felt at a distinct disadvantage. Nevertheless, she matched the woman, tone for tone.

"Why, Mrs. Stonewell, I am surprised you do not see the advantages to yourself of your lodgers having callers. After all, the more people who see this house, the more people who might choose to obtain lodgings here on their own behalf, would you not think?"

That gave the landlady pause but then she shook her head, "Not callers such as that," she said with a sniff. "And you have done more than enough in that department anyway," she added tartly. "I cannot spend all my day catering to people who come to see you!"

With that, she turned and walked away. Marian fled to her room.

Penelope and Geoffrey reached Bath after a journey that was more rapid than was usual for them. No stopping, on this trip, to visit scholars along the way. No hopping out of the carriage to ooh and ahh over a site that would be perfect for their experiments.

No, this time they directed the coachman to drive straight to Bath to the York House Inn. The moment their things were taken upstairs, unpacked, and they had changed, they decided to call upon Lady Merriweather. After they spoke to her, then they would call upon Miss Tibbles.

There was no question that Lady Merriweather would receive them. She was delighted, as she said, to welcome to Bath Mrs. Talbot, the niece of her bosom bow, Lady Brisbane. And the niece's husband.

She was also, it seemed, eager to unburden herself of her grievances toward a certain person who seemed to have set herself up far above her station!

"Miss Tibbles?" Penelope echoed the name with a sinking heart.

"Yes. Miss Tibbles! A mere governess. And she has the audacity to think herself a worthy bride for my nephew. Can you imagine anything more absurd?" Lady Merriweather sputtered.

"Yes, but my understanding is that Miss Tibbles is of perfectly respectable birth," Geoffrey pointed out, as gently as he could.

Lady Merriweather sniffed. "That is neither here nor there. She has been in service for these past twenty years and that is more than enough to alter her circumstances irretrievably. And that is another point," she said, gathering steam. "The woman is past her last prayers! How dare she seek to entrap my nephew?"

But this was too much for Penelope. She bristled. "It has only been eighteen years and Miss Tibbles would not entrap anyone," she snapped.

Lady Merriweather looked affronted and Geoffrey hastily intervened. "Tell us more about your nephew, Lady Merriweather," he said. "I understand the colonel has only recently sold out his commission. Did he see much action? Was he with Wellington at Waterloo?"

Now this was a subject dear to Lady Merriweather's heart and she was quite content to elaborate on her nephew's merits for some time. She waxed eloquent about his bravery. She spoke of the honors heaped upon his shoulders. She spoke of his intelligence and common sense.

"Your nephew sounds as if he is a most remarkable man," Geoffrey said politely, when he was finally able to interject a word or two.

"Oh, he is," Lady Merriweather assured them.

"I wonder then how you can so underrate him," Penelope said sweetly.

Lady Merriweather looked taken aback. "I? Underrate him? Surely you are mistaken!"

"Well, you say he is intelligent and has a great deal of common sense, but you do not trust him to know what is in his own best interest," Penelope persisted, in the same sweet voice as before.

Lady Merriweather's eyes narrowed and she glared at Penelope. She opened her mouth to speak and closed it again, unable to easily think of a way to refute the argument. Finally she did so.

In a voice that was as falsely sweet as Penelope's, she said, "It is just that after Merriweather's disastrous first marriage, I wish him to be happy. And even a sensible man may be taken in by a brazen hussy!"

Both Penelope and Geoffrey were too taken aback by the vivid image of Miss Tibbles portrayed as a brazen hussy to instantly reply. Indeed, it was an image that held such appeal, for its absurdity, that they did not wish to rapidly relinquish it. Reluctantly they did so."

Tell us more about the colonel's first marriage," Geoffrey suggested. "Was it a long one?"

But Lady Merriweather appeared to regret having even mentioned it. She clamped her lips tightly together and refused to say anything more on the subject.

Geoffrey tried to probe delicately as to the state of Colonel Merriweather's financial position. That set up Lady Merriweather's back even more.

"My nephew is not a fortune hunter," she said. "I don't care what anyone may say! The very fact that he is considering marriage to this, this governess proves that. It is beyond everything to hear such nonsense! And I strongly advise you to ignore any gossip you may hear about his first wife's death as well. There is not the least bit of truth to it, I am certain."

All of which was more than enough to cause Penelope and Geoffrey to regard one another with wide eyes. They did try a few more discreet questions but it became clear that nothing more was to be learned. However belatedly, Lady Merriweather had now decided on discretion.

So, reluctantly, as soon as they politely could do so, after answering her questions about Lady Brisbane and Lord and Lady Westcott and the Westcott girls, all now happily married, as well as about Miss Tibbles, Penelope and Geoffrey made their escape.

"She has her own plans for Colonel Merriweather," Penelope said thoughtfully as they walked toward the part of town where Miss Tibbles was staying. "That is why she objects so strongly to the match."

"What are you talking about?" Geoffrey asked, bewildered.

Penelope smiled up at her husband as she tucked her hand into his elbow. "Lady Merriweather. I have no doubt she has been matchmaking."

"Do you not think," he countered cautiously, "that it is just as she said? That she wishes her nephew to marry better? Not," he added hastily, "that I think anyone could do better than Miss Tibbles. However, from a worldly point of view, it is quite different."

Penelope sniffed. "Perhaps. But if this Colonel Merriweather cries off because his aunt dislikes the match, then he is a fool."

Talbot rubbed the side of his nose. "Undoubtedly," he agreed cautiously. "But Penelope? Do we want him to marry Miss Tibbles? There are a number of things we have heard that sound distinctly havey-cavey."

Now her shoulders slumped. "No, of course we do not," she agreed with a sigh. "It is just that I should so dearly love to see Miss Tibbles happy and I cannot bear it when anyone looks down upon her. Particularly when they do so because she has been a governess."

"I know, dearest," Geoffrey said, patting her hand, "I know."

Colonel Merriweather was not surprised when the landlady at Miss Tibbles' lodgings wished to pull him aside and speak with him. He had long since realized she was wholly on his side in his courtship attempt. He was, however, surprised at what she had to tell him.

"A seedy fellow, very seedy, came to call on her this morning," Mrs. Stonewell said with a sniff.

"A relative down on his luck, perhaps," Andrew suggested lightly.

"You may jest of it, but I don't," Mrs. Stonewell retorted. "You may not know it, but Miss Tibbles is not paying the bills here herself. It is her last employer, the Earl of Westcott, who arranged everything for her to have a holiday in Bath. It's my belief the fellow this morning was a creditor, come to dun her for payment of some bill."

Andrew started to object but could not. It was, after all, quite possible that Miss Tibbles had come to *point non plus*. The salary of a governess was not precisely generous and it would not at all be surprising if she had outspent her purse.

"Well, well, I shall look into the matter," he promised the landlady. Then, he said with a gentle smile, "I am certain that you know what it is like to not be as beforehand with the world as you would like."

"Well, there have been times when I have been obliged

to practice economies," Mrs. Stonewell grudgingly agreed. "And so long as her bill has been paid here, I have no quarrel with Miss Tibbles, I suppose. She is certainly respectable enough in her own person. But I will not have such men hanging about my establishment! It doesn't look right."

"I quite understand," he agreed soothingly. "And I shall tell Miss Tibbles that if she should happen to have creditors dunning her, that she may send them to me. I should be happy to settle with them."

He paused and leaned closer to the landlady, who was eyeing him with some suspicion. "You must have guessed that it is my dearest wish that circumstances should shortly make it entirely my province to settle Miss Tibbles' debts. I am hopeful, indeed all but certain, that before the year is out, Miss Tibbles will agree to be my wife. But," he added, putting a finger to his lips, "you must not say a word to anyone. Yet. I have not completely persuaded Miss Tibbles and you know how malicious some gossipmongers can be."

Mrs. Stonewell agreed that she did indeed know. And that she would take it upon herself to send any seedy characters directly to the colonel should any of them have the effrontery to call at the lodging house again.

"Capital!" Andrew said, beaming his approval. "I knew I could depend upon your good sense. And your discretion. Now, if you would tell Miss Tibbles I am here, I should be very much obliged."

Since the colonel then also winked at her and pressed a coin in her hand, the landlady hastened to do as he asked, assuring herself that she was assisting with a marvelous romance.

And indeed it gave one hope. If a governess could marry a gentleman as nicely turned out and with such handsome manners as the colonel, why there might even be hope for someone who ran a genteel boardinghouse in Bath.

With pleasant daydreams running through her mind, Mrs. Stonewell hastened her step and rapped smartly on Miss Tibbles' door. If she seemed more cordial than she had in the morning, the governess did not mention it. She merely thanked the landlady, with becoming reserve, and collected her bonnet, reticule, and spencer before following her downstairs.

There Mrs. Stonewell observed what seemed to her to be a most affecting meeting between the governess and the colonel. There was something so romantic about the way Colonel Merriweather took her gloved hand in his and raised it to his lips. Something so becoming about the way Miss Tibbles blushed and tried to hide her smile. It was not as though matters went any further. Not in her house, for she ran a most respectable boarding establishment.

Oh, yes, Mrs. Stonewell had no doubt that the colonel had the right of it when he said they would be married before the year was out. Smelling of April and May they were, the both of them.

She continued to watch as Colonel Merriweather tucked Miss Tibbles' hand under his arm and they strolled down the street looking, for all the world, as if they were the only two people on it. She let out a sigh. It really was, she had to admit, the most romantic thing that she had ever seen!

Chapter 13

Penelope and Geoffrey eyed the landlady with some disfavor. She returned the compliment in full measure. She sniffed.

"No, I do not know when Miss Tibbles will return, but I do not expect that it will be for some time."

"I see. I suppose you cannot tell us, either, where she might be, where she might have gone?" Geoffrey asked.

"It is not my business to pry into the lives of the ladies staying under my roof," Mrs. Stonewell replied primly.

Since Geoffrey had failed to elicit any useful information, Penelope decided to try her hand at doing so. She sighed and smiled at the landlady wistfully.

"I don't suppose, then, that you can tell us, either, if she was with Colonel Merriweather? His aunt, dear Lady Merriweather, told us they have taken an interest in one another."

The mere mention of his name produced the most amazing transformation in the woman. She smiled and leaned forward and said, "So you are friends of the colonel as well? That puts an entirely different complexion on the matter. Isn't it the most wonderful thing?"

Within moments, Penelope and the landlady were deep in conversation about the budding romance and Geoffrey could only watch in bemusement.

*   *   *

Miss Tibbles was tired when the colonel finally returned her to her lodgings and he left her with a bow and concern in his eyes.

"You must ask Mrs. Stonewell to bring you up some tea," he told her. "And then lie down on your bed for a while. You are not yet recovered, I can see."

That was not it, but Marian could scarcely tell him so. Not when it would mean admitting he was the cause of the ache in her head.

She still didn't know what to make of him. Or of what the Runner had told her. Her head told her to be wary. Her heart told her to love. As matters stood, it seemed she could not do either. Or, rather, she could not help but do both.

So severe was her headache, that Marian could only view with a sinking heart Mrs. Stonewell coming toward her, a knowing look on her face. Her next words made her spirits sink even further.

"You've visitors. Again. I've put them in the parlor."

"Thank you."

"Shall I have tea sent in?" Mrs. Stonewell persisted.

That startled Marian. It was the first time the landlady had offered such a gesture toward anyone who had come to call upon her, and there had been several former charges or their mamas who had done so since she arrived in Bath. These must be very special guests, indeed, to have captured Mrs. Stonewell's fancy so.

"Yes, thank you, that would be very kind," she said, trying to keep her voice from betraying her surprise.

The landlady's next words told her why she was behaving with such kindness. She leaned toward Marian and said, in a conspiratorial voice, "They are friends of Colonel Merriweather as well as friends of yours, you know."

More bewildered than ever, for she could not imagine

who the common acquaintances could be, she headed for the parlor. And came to a dead stop in the doorway.

"Penelope? Mr. Talbot?" she said with some surprise.

Penelope instantly came forward to hug her and Miss Tibbles was too dazed to even think to reprove her. Mr. Talbot merely smiled ruefully.

Marian blurted out the first thought that came to her mind. "I didn't know you knew Colonel Merriweather!"

Mr. Talbot looked toward the door, careful to make certain no one was in earshot, then closed it and said to Miss Tibbles, softly, "We don't. But we allowed the landlady to think so and it warmed her greatly toward us."

"Please don't scold Geoffrey," Penelope said anxiously. "Truly she was so brisk with us that it was the only thing we could think of to make her thaw. And she did."

"Of course," Marian said, taking a seat as far from the door as possible so perforce the others did as well. After this morning she was taking no chances of being overheard. "I am of little consequence compared to Colonel Merriweather. Oh, I don't blame her, it is the way of the world, after all. But why am I prattling on about such nonsense? I presume you have seen the solicitor and come to tell me what you discovered about my inheritance? If there even is an inheritance, that is."

"Oh, there is," Penelope assured her. "Quite a nice little one. It has apparently been waiting for you for eight years."

"Eight years?" Marian echoed, hearing herself as though from a distance.

Eight years. For eight years she might have been able to live quietly. For eight years she need not have been in service.

Abruptly she realized that Penelope was regarding her with a stricken look in her eyes and realized that she, too, was thinking they might never have known each other.

Marian immediately, instinctively, gathered her wits about her and said lightly, "How astonishing. But then, had I known, I would never have met the family that has become dearest to me of all the ones I have ever worked for."

It was the right thing to say. Marian knew it the moment she saw Penelope's eyes light up with relief. Still, she needed to know more. She plied the two with questions and they answered as readily as they could. They had, it seemed, thought to ask all the questions she would have done and perhaps even a few more.

There was something they were not telling her. Some point they were concerned about but not quite certain how to tell her. This diffidence annoyed Marian. She told them so, quite pithily, and was pleased to see by their guilty expressions that she had not been mistaken.

"Well, there is something more we learned," Geoffrey began.

"But not in detail," Penelope added hastily.

"Mere gossip, perhaps."

"But perhaps you ought to know."

"What. Is. It?"

"Colonel Merriweather. He did go to see the solicitor about your inheritance. And he may have murdered his first wife!"

Marian knew that she had gone very white. "Who told you so?"

"His aunt and the solicitor," Penelope answered miserably.

"To be precise," Geoffrey corrected her, "the solicitor told us that the colonel had inquired after your inheritance. And Lady Merriweather said we must pay absolutely no attention to any rumors about his first wife's death. It was someone else who told us that there are those who believe he murdered her."

Marian felt herself go very cold. She could not help

thinking of the sheaf of notes, upstairs in her room, still unread, that the Runner had given her. How was she to answer Geoffrey and Penelope?

But she didn't need to answer them. They were not in the least surprised that she should be stunned by their news, for they presumed it was the first she had heard of it. They rushed on to tell her precisely what they thought she ought to do.

"You must break things off with Colonel Merriweather straight away," Penelope said.

"Indeed?" Marian replied, her voice at its frostiest.

"Yes, and perhaps even leave Bath. We cannot think it would be wise for you to remain here, Miss Tibbles. We shall take you back to London with us and, once you claim your inheritance, we shall help you find a snug little cottage. Perhaps on one of our estates. Between my sisters and myself and Mama and Papa and Aunt Ariana, there must be a suitable one somewhere."

Marian tried to imagine such a future for herself. To her amazement, she discovered it was a surprisingly disconcerting picture. And a very depressing one.

Nor did she like being in the position of having someone else tell her what to do. Particularly not a chit of a girl who, while she might be married, was not so very long out of the schoolroom, after all.

Geoffrey apparently read enough of her feelings from her expression that he reached out to touch Penelope's arm. But his wife, once begun, could not easily be halted from her course.

"We must take you away from here as soon as possible, Miss Tibbles. I am certain you must be unaware, but you have become the talk of Bath. And it looks so foolish for a woman of your age to be behaving in such a particular way!"

"A woman of my age?" Marian repeated in a dangerous voice. "In such a particular way?"

Penelope nodded warily. Miss Tibbles rose to her feet and advanced upon the young woman. "I thank you for your concern, my dear! After all, as feeble and lacking in wits as I seem to have become, what would I do, what could I do, without your wisdom and counsel?"

"I, that is to say, really, Miss Tibbles, I meant no slight to you," Penelope protested, shrinking back against the chair she sat upon.

"No?" Marian demanded. "Nevertheless you seem to have forgotten that it is my life which is at issue here. Mine! And that I have shown sufficient wit and wisdom to manage it tolerably well thus far."

She paused and drew in a breath but it was only to continue the attack. "I thank you for visiting the solicitor as I asked. I even thank you, I think, for your concern in visiting Lady Merriweather. I do not thank you, however, for attempting to tell me how to live my life."

"But surely you do not mean to continue to see the colonel, after what we have learned of him?" Geoffrey protested.

It had been a long, troubling day, the only part of which had held any happiness for her being the time she spent in Andrew's company. No matter what her head told her, Miss Tibbles' heart could not bear to turn away from him. So now she rounded, instead, on Talbot.

"No?" she demanded. "Not only do I intend to continue to see Colonel Merriweather, but I may even go dancing with him. Waltzing, perhaps! And if anyone dislikes it, well, it is just too bad."

And with that, Miss Tibbles stormed from the room, not caring whether Penelope and Geoffrey stayed or went. Nor did she pause as she nearly bowled over the landlady in the hallway. Indeed, she did not stop for any reason until she had reached the safety and privacy of her room, where she shut and locked the door.

Only then did she allow herself to give way to all the

emotions she felt. She flung herself in the chair by the
window, watching the people go by, down below. Before
her, locked in her writing desk, was the sheaf of papers
from the Runner. She would need to look at them, she
knew, but not just yet. Instead she did her best not to give
way to the blue devils that were plaguing her.

The truth be told, Marian was appalled by her behavior. How could she have rounded on Penelope and her
husband so? They were only trying to help and had said
only what was sensible. And yet Miss Tibbles would not
take back a single word of what she had said, even if she
could.

That was what appalled Marian the most. That such a
short time in Bath, spent in the company of Colonel Merriweather, could cause her to so far forget her principles
that she could speak as she had to Penelope. That she
could threaten to cause even more gossip than she already
had. And, even worse, to mean it.

For despite all her promises to herself to be sensible, to
walk away from Andrew, if need be, she could not do it,
no matter what the gossips said of him. No matter what
the papers the Runner brought her said.

She would be careful, she would be wary of actually
marrying the man, but she would not walk away. Not yet.
First she would dream a little longer, let herself pretend,
just a little longer, that it was not impossible for her to be
in love, for her to find happiness with this man.

Had it been one of her charges behaving so foolishly,
Miss Tibbles would not have tolerated such nonsense.
She wondered that she could tolerate it in herself. But,
wonder or not, apparently she could and was.

A tiny smile even crept across her face as she imagined
herself dancing at the next Bath assembly, perhaps even
waltzing in Colonel Merriweather's arms. It was an
image which brought a blush to her cheeks and an unac-
customed warmth to her heart. But she would not banish

it for the world. Not when it could make her feel so young again.

Still, some semblance of the old Miss Tibbles re-mained. Enough to keep her from consigning the papers the Runner had given her to the fire. She would keep them. She just wouldn't read them. At least not yet.

Not until she had letters back from the girls and the families of girls she had once been governess for. Not until she had something other than one man's opinion with which to compare what she was told.

Marian was a cynical woman. She was at heart also a romantic one. She had long known the first; the second came as a surprise and one she would have, a year earlier, denied as absurd.

She could not deny it anymore.

Chapter 14

Colonel Merriweather was surprised but very, very pleased when Miss Tibbles consented to go to a ball at the New Assembly rooms with him. He did not ask what had changed her mind. It was better, he thought, not to risk tempting fate by asking her.

In his eyes, Marian looked beautiful. Her hair was arranged in curls that framed her face and she wore the rose silk gown again that became her so well. She had pearls in her ears and clasped around her throat and soft slippers that peeped out from beneath her gown as she walked.

But the greatest difference seemed to be in the way she carried herself. No one, who did not already know, would have guessed she was or had been a governess. Her back was straight, she smiled as though she had not a care in the world, and there was a gaiety about her he had never seen before.

Andrew found himself thinking that tonight he was a very lucky man. Marian could not outshine, of course, the girls making their first come-out. She had long since lost that first blush of youth. But there was a wisdom, a kindness, a certainty of character that he found infinitely more alluring, and so he told her as she walked by his side to the assembly rooms.

She shook her head, but could not hide the smile that

quivered despite all her best attempts to keep him from seeing it.

It was a grave error, a mistake, to agree to attend a ball at the New Assembly rooms. Marian knew it. To be sure, it would have been far worse in London, but she knew she would be regarded as an upstart who was trying to appear above her station.

Still she went. She would be grave. She would move with dignity. She would do nothing, other than attend, which could draw censure down upon her head. Those were the resolutions with which Miss Tibbles armed herself. Until she entered the assembly rooms.

The room was crowded. It was a very long time since she had found herself part of such a gathering. She found herself grateful that she was here with Colonel Merriweather by her side for even she would otherwise have found it a trifle daunting.

And yet, there was something that called to her across the years. Something that reminded her, as though it were yesterday, of her own Season in London. First one corner of her mouth quirked upward, and then the other, and before she knew it, Marian was laughing. She moved with a lightness she thought she had forgotten. She carried herself with an assurance of a young girl who knows she is sought after. And when Colonel Merriweather smiled down at her, she did not trouble to hide the glow in her eyes.

There was Penelope, clutching Mr. Talbot's arm, and staring at Marian as if she could not believe her eyes. Good! Let her know that Miss Tibbles was not about to be dictated to by a mere chit of a girl.

She smiled up at Colonel Merriweather and she heard him catch his breath in the most gratifying way. Her hand tightened, just the slightest little bit on his arm, and his eyes glittered down at her even more.

"Shall we dance?" he asked.

Marian hesitated. For all her vaunted courage in accepting his invitation to this ball, for all her vows to Penelope that she meant to waltz, she felt herself falter now. Did she truly dare? But it wasn't a waltz. It was a country dance that was forming and surely that would be unexceptionable?

She looked up at Colonel Merriweather. "I should like it very much," she said.

He led her to where the couples were forming the lines for the country dance and he smiled so warmly at her that Marian wished she had a fan to cool herself. But that would have created even more of a spectacle than the colonel's open admiration, the mere action of a fan drawing eyes to her face, noticing the governess who dared to behave as if she belonged here. She would simply have to endure.

Ah, there was the music now. A bow, a curtsy, a meeting of hands and a graceful circle to the left. Marian had forgotten how much such simple steps meant to her. How they lifted her spirits and caused her to smile. How easily the steps came back to her so that she missed not a single beat. Nor did the colonel. Andrew was as graceful a dancer as she had ever seen.

To her left and to her right, Marian could see some of the young ladies experimenting with outlandish turns and movements of their feet. Colonel Merriweather frowned in patent disapproval as one damsel exposed far more of her ankle than was seemly. Indeed, he fairly bristled with indignation.

"What the deuce is the matter with her?" he demanded in a fierce whisper when the figure of the dance brought him close enough to Marian to ask without being overheard. "Is the poor girl having a fit?"

She smiled fondly. She knew. Oh, yes, she knew. Her last charge, before she had taken on the care of the Westcott girls, had tried to make just such a spectacle of herself at Almack's. Miss Tibbles had managed to prevent it.

When the dancing brought them back close enough for her to answer discreetly, she said, "I collect the girl persuaded her father to hire an opera dancer to teach her. She is only imitating, and badly at that, I fear, what she has seen. It has been a common fashion, these past few years here at home, but one I have done my best to discourage with the girls under my care."

The colonel's muttered exclamation did not quite reach Marian's ears and upon consideration, she decided it was probably just as well.

Even as she smiled at the girl who was still making a spectacle of herself, Marian also felt her heart lurch, just a little. This was precisely the sort of impetuous child she would likely have had to deal with next, if there had been no inheritance. As she would still have to deal with if the inheritance turned out to be merely a hum, some sort of mistake.

Then she would again find herself dealing with girls like this one. And just now, dancing as she was, Marian could not imagine herself doing so. She could not imagine finding the strength, finding the patience, to school such a girl to the propriety that her parents, and the *ton,* would demand of her.

She wanted to believe it would never come to that but, despite her defiance in coming here tonight with Andrew, Marian knew it still might. If the charges against him were true. If her inheritance proved to be less than Penelope understood the solicitor to say it would be. If somehow something happened to her funds.

The music drew to a close. Another bow, another curtsy, then she was taking Colonel Merriweather's arm as he led her off the dance floor.

"I believe someone is signaling to you," Andrew murmured softly.

Marian looked in the direction he was gazing and saw that both Penelope and her husband, Mr. Talbot, were regarding her with patent disapproval and Penelope forgot herself so far as to actually gesture to her to come to them.

Her spine stiffened. For a tuppence she would have spun on her heel and walked in the opposite direction. But no one offered her a tuppence and the assembly room was monstrously crowded and it seemed easier, after all, to get this meeting over with. Then perhaps she could dance again.

Indeed, she did not make it to the Talbots before a gentleman, the gentleman she had met the first day she met Colonel Merriweather, came up and greeted the colonel and asked Marian to dance. With ill grace the colonel relinquished her into Major Hainesly's care.

Marian could not help it, but she felt a twinge of vindication and triumph as she saw the look of chagrin on Penelope's face. Well, the poor child must just get used to the notion that her old governess might still be found a desirable dance partner by members of the opposite sex.

Major Hainesly was just as accomplished a dancer as Colonel Merriweather and Marian commented upon that fact to him. He grimaced, then grinned. "Any officer who has ever served on Wellington's staff must be. He often told us that he thought half the diplomatic battles were won on the dance floor. And that the best intelligence sources were often to be found among the ladies there."

They were separated by the dance and when they came together again, the major sighed dramatically. "It was a difficult and dangerous duty, but Merriweather and I screwed up our courage and did what we had to do."

Marian laughed. "And did it marvelously well, too," she told him approvingly.

Major Hainesly smiled. "You have laughing eyes," he

said. "It makes you look so young. No wonder Merriweather is head over heels for you."

She blushed, not knowing what to say or even how to meet his eyes. But he seemed to understand and besides the figure of the dance was separating them again. Marian tried to focus on something else, tried to regain her composure before she had to face Hainesly again.

But she need not have worried. The perfect gentleman, he spoke lightly of other things and she managed to answer creditably. And when they were done he bowed, she curtsied, and he said, "I should escort you back to Merriweather but I fear you are about to receive other offers to dance."

And she did. There were an astonishing number of retired military gentlemen in Bath, it seemed, and they all wanted to dance with her, for word seemed to have gone from one to another of who she was.

But when the musicians struck up the first chords of the waltz, Marian refused the gentleman who solicited her hand for it and looked for Andrew. He did not fail her. Suddenly he was there, bowing, holding out his hand to her. She placed her hand in his and together they glided onto the floor and took their place among the swirling couples.

She had never danced the waltz before, never thought to dance the waltz. And yet she had watched, secretly yearning, when her pupils had been taught. In private she had practiced alone, humming to herself, and pretending she had a partner. But this was far more wonderful than she had ever been able to imagine, far more scandalous in how close she was to a man. In short, it was a dance that might have been designed for her, and Marian found herself wishing it might never end. She looked up at Andrew to see if he found it as wonderful as she did and was taken aback by what she saw.

There was a hint of sternness in his eyes as he looked

down at her. "General Elston," he said, naming her last
partner, "only made general because his family bought
him his first commission while he was still in the nursery."

Marian smiled mischievously. "But his merits on the
dance floor are clearly his own."

The sternness became a forbidding glower. "Trying to
make me jealous?" Andrew demanded angrily. "I had
best tell you straightaway that I will not play games with
you."

That startled Marian. She pulled slightly away so that
she could look up at him, but not so far as to make an ob-
vious spectacle of herself.

"Indeed not!" she exclaimed indignantly. "I have neither been playing games nor attempting to make you jealous. I have been shielding both our reputations. We may
not be in our first blush of youth but I assure you that
were I to dance only with you it would cause an excessive amount of unpleasant gossip. And rightly so!"

His gaze softened then. "Oh, to the devil," he muttered.
"I wish you were betrothed to me. And that I had the right
to keep you by my side the entire evening."

He looked so fierce that Marian could not resist roasting him, just a little. "Ah, but, my dear Colonel Merriweather, that would occasion even more gossip. A couple
who were so fond of one another they could not bear to
be apart? How absurd! How unfashionable!" She paused
and her voice dropped low, so low he could scarcely hear
her as she whispered, "How wonderful."

But he did hear her. His grip on her waist tightened. "It
would be wonderful," he echoed fiercely. "And one day I
hope it will be so for us!"

It was nonsense. She ought to deal him a setdown for
such impertinence but, oh, how wonderful it was to hear
such things and Marian found she could not bear to rep-
rimand him for saying them. Instead she turned the talk

to other things and when the waltz ended, allowed him finally to take her over to the Talbots.

Marian braced herself for a tirade. Penelope had not been happy before and she no doubt had worked herself into a towering rage as her governess had managed to evade her for so great a part of the evening. When they were almost there, she turned to the colonel and said, "Perhaps I had best speak to them alone."

He nodded, bowed, and released her. Marian smiled. This was one of the things that made the man so dear to her.

Another gentleman immediately appeared, offering to dance with her, and blocking the way to where the Talbots stood waiting. Marian smiled but shook her head.

"Forgive me, sir," she said, "but I fear the waltz has left me out of breath and I see friends I must speak to."

He retreated with good grace and she swallowed a tiny sigh of relief. Dancing again with Andrew had reminded her of the difference, for her, between him and all of the other men present.

But she must not think of that now. Here was Penelope. Strange, she didn't look to be in a towering rage. Still, Marian was wary. Particularly as, now that she was alone, she noticed the curious glances cast her way and the whispering going on around her. It was foolish to think it must all be about her and yet she did stand out. There must be many who wondered who had the audacity to act, at her age, as if she were a young miss in her first Season.

Miss Tibbles finally reached the Talbots. Mr. Talbot was grinning at her. "Why, Miss Tibbles, I didn't know you had permission to waltz."

"Don't be impertinent!" she snapped, but her eyes seemed to smile at him anyway, sharing the jest.

"You do truly love him, don't you?" Penelope asked, a worried look in her eyes.

Marian nodded, unable to speak, conscious that too many curious ears might be interested in anything she said.

Penelope sighed. "Well, I cannot say that we like it, this connection with a man who has so many unanswered questions about him, but I am glad you have found happiness, at least for a little while, however long it may last."

"Thank you, I think," Marian said dryly.

Lady Merriweather clenched her fan tightly in her hands. The Talbots had done nothing, she thought, to detach this Miss Tibbles from Andrew's clutches. The way he looked at her tonight, and she at him, proved as much. Very well, she would have to take action herself.

Lady Merriweather hoped she was a charitable woman, but to see her favorite nephew throw himself away on a mere nobody like Miss Tibbles was not to be borne. He must be made to see the folly of his ways!

Others were watching as well. Now that Andrew had flaunted the woman, positively flaunted the woman, before all their acquaintances, for this was far more revealing than the musicale had been, it was useless to pretend. Cordelia would have to acknowledge the connection, however much she disliked doing so.

She looked about her. Someone here must be able to help her, but who? Her eyes fell on a young man, a handsome young man, newly come into a fortune. He had the face of an angel and the soul, she had heard, of the devil. The source of his fortune was said to be an uncanny knack at cards, a knack some stopped barely short of calling cheating, and an intimate knowledge, others said, of the secrets of powerful men and women.

He would, Lady Merriweather decided, be perfect. She had no doubt that for the right price he would do as she asked. And he was handsome enough to be able to tempt any woman, even, she hoped, Miss Tibbles.

Lady Merriweather suppressed a twinge of guilt over what she planned to do. After all, her notion would work only if Miss Tibbles was as foolish or as grasping as Lady Merriweather suspected her to be. If she was indeed constant in her affections, why then the plan would have not the slightest effect at all.

With a smile that would have alarmed anyone who knew her well, Lady Merriweather moved toward the young man. With the instincts of his sort, he sensed her coming and turned to greet her with a polished bow and a quirked eyebrow of inquiry.

"My dear Mr. Cunnington, I understand we have some mutual friends. Pray give me your arm and walk around the room a bit while we talk."

His expression became even more puzzled but he did as she asked and that, Lady Merriweather told herself, was a very good sign indeed.

Chapter 15

Only the most select of company was invited to Lady Merriweather's little soirée. The highest sticklers. And Mr. Cunnington. And Miss Tibbles.

"To bring your fiancée to the notice of Bath's most esteemed citizens," Lady Merriweather explained when Andrew asked, with narrowed eyes, why his aunt was throwing her party and why she had invited Marian.

Andrew was wary. He was downright suspicious. But how could he refuse? It was a wonderful opportunity to bring Marian into favor. No doubt his aunt expected Marian to find herself overwhelmed by the company. If so, she didn't know his beloved very well.

So Colonel Merriweather called for Miss Tibbles and accompanied her back to his aunt's house on the evening in question. She looked wonderful, he thought. She had splurged on a new gown, a soft blue edging into teal, and it suited her admirably.

She regarded him calmly and if she still kept something of a distance between them, well, Andrew was prepared to acknowledge that it was proper she do so. Particularly tonight when their behavior would be under such close scrutiny. He said something of the sort aloud.

Marian laughed and yet, it seemed to him, there was a hesitancy in her laugh. Was she perhaps truly worried? He tried to tease her out of it.

"Afraid my aunt will overwhelm you?"

She looked at him frankly. "Not your aunt, perhaps, but I am certain her guests were chosen to show me how very much out of place I shall be if I marry you. And I am not entirely certain she is wrong in saying so."

"Nonsense!" Andrew squeezed her hand reassuringly. "You have dealt with far worse than a few old biddies! Why, the least of the girls you had in hand would seem to be far more daunting than anyone my aunt could possibly conjure up to be here tonight."

She smiled but shook her head. Gruffly he told her, "Well, at all events, I don't care. I want you here, tonight, by my side, and I shall be very proud that you are. And if anyone tries to overset you I shall send them to the rightabout!"

Unfortunately, his Aunt Cordelia had other plans. She had not planned this evening in order for Andrew to act as Miss Tibbles' protector. Not long after they arrived, she managed to find an excuse to separate them, sending Andrew on some errand a servant could just as easily have carried out. But he went. Whatever her motives, just having Marian here, tonight, would do much to make his marriage to her more acceptable to the *ton*.

The moment her nephew was out of earshot, Lady Merriweather turned to Miss Tibbles and said, "I suppose I must accept you into the family. It is not a decision I like but I suppose I have no choice."

Marian had learned a good many years ago, in her first post, to tell when someone was lying to her. Had she not been able to do so, she would have been a singular failure as a governess.

But she could. And by the way Lady Merriweather evaded her eyes, by the way her lips twitched as she spoke, by the pitch of her voice, Marian knew the woman was endeavoring to deceive her. The only question was what her purpose really was in giving this party and inviting the woman she did not wish her nephew to marry.

But Marian betrayed none of her thoughts. A governess could not afford to do so, not if she wished to keep her post. So she merely said, gravely, "You are very kind, Lady Merriweather."

"If you find yourself overwhelmed by the company, as I suppose you might, after all your years *in service,* pray do not hesitate to withdraw early. I assure you I shall understand perfectly!"

And with those cutting words, Lady Merriweather moved away. They ought to have explained everything. Indeed, they confirmed her own suspicions, spoken to Colonel Merriweather earlier. But some tingling in her spine told Marian there was still more to it than that.

But she did not allow herself to dwell on the matter. Time, and careful observation, she was sure, would provide the answer.

So Marian mingled with the other guests. She rather expected to be ignored and to have some turn away as she approached. She soon discovered her error. They preferred to see themselves as hounds on the hunt with Marian as their quarry.

Between the falsely sweet questions as to her family and what was it that had happened to her father? Or mock innocent questions as to whether she was here to look for a new employer, Marian might well have found herself overset. Except for Mr. Cunnington.

He rescued her from one particularly nasty encounter by the simple expedience of placing a glass in her hand, taking her arm, and swinging her out of the circle she found herself in.

Only when they were several steps away, out of earshot, did he speak.

"My deepest apologies. I perhaps ought not to have done that, but you looked in need of rescuing and I was taught always to come to the aid of a lady. May I introduce myself? I am Robert Cunnington. The Honorable Robert Cunnington, though that seems rather irrelevant."

Marian studied the man before her. He was elegantly dressed, within a year or two of her own age, she would have guessed, and he carried himself with an air of consequence and assurance that argued he had both wealth and breeding. And yet there was something more. Something she did not entirely trust.

Still, she smiled at him, though the smile did not quite reach her eyes. "I thank you for your gallant rescue," she said, a hint of reserve in her voice. "I am Miss Marian Tibbles."

"Ah, that explains it then."

"Explains it?" Marian echoed warily.

"You are the governess who has the temerity to think you can marry one of us!"

"It has been done before," she said with a sniff.

"Yes, by a pretty young thing who had been a governess only a short time. One who had not yet had time to forget what it was like to be a lady." He smiled and tacitly invited her to share that smile. He lowered his voice as he went on, in a conspiratorial tone, "Don't you know that anything might be forgiven youth and beauty?"

"And nothing forgiven age and wisdom," Marian retorted tartly.

He shrugged. "I did not say I approved, I merely explained what is happening. There are too many changes going on in our world. People are afraid the lines will blur between servant and mistress. Already some I know are trying to make the distinctions greater and I fear it will only become more so."

"What was I supposed to do?" Marian demanded tartly. "If not a governess then what?"

"Why, abide in genteel poverty, of course," he said as though surprised she did not know it. "Had you languished in genteel poverty, all these years, there would have been far less of a problem."

"Genteel poverty?" Marian snapped. "A burden to any relative who might reluctantly take me in? I thank you but I think not!"

He shrugged. Then he smiled again. "I have made you angry and I swear I did not mean to do so. I have turned out to be a very poor rescuer indeed."

Mr. Cunnington looked so blue-deviled, so contrite, that in spite of herself Marian found herself reassuring him. She placed a hand on his arm, when he would have turned away, and said, "You have at least tried and for that I am grateful, sir."

He smiled back at her and placed his own hand over hers. He pressed her hand gently and then, just as Marian was about to pull free, a voice from behind her said, indignantly, "Let go of my fiancée!"

Instantly Cunnington let go, pulling away as if he had been scalded. And Marian blushed as she snatched her hand away from his arm. But she turned to Andrew and said, with quiet dignity, "Mr. Cunnington came to my rescue and I was only thanking him."

Now Andrew colored up but did not entirely relent. "My apologies, Mr. Cunnington, and I thank you for taking the trouble on my fiancée's behalf. I can take care of her now however."

Cunnington waved a hand airily. "Think nothing of it. Nothing at all. Entirely my pleasure to be of service to such a charming lady."

And then he bowed and retreated, leaving Marian and Andrew alone. Or rather, as alone as they could be in the midst of his aunt's gathering.

They smiled at one another, albeit a trifle hesitantly.

"There you are!" a voice intruded.

Both Merriweather and Marian turned to see who was

speaking. Immediately she smiled very widely and said, "Lady Wyndham! How very nice to see you here!"

The woman approaching smiled just as broadly. "Put the cat among the pigeons, have you, Miss Tibbles? Quite the opposite of the advice you used to give my granddaughter, Amelia."

Merriweather cleared his throat in a warning manner but the woman waved her hand at him. "No need to take snuff at me, boy. I'm not objecting to what the pair of you choose to do. Always said Miss Tibbles was a lady and had sense. Think you've done very well for yourself."

As this was directed at the colonel, Marian laughed. "That is not precisely the general view here tonight."

"Pish tosh!" Lady Wyndham exclaimed. "Don't listen to a one of them. I shall have something to say about whether you are accepted in Bath or not and I say you shall be."

"You are very good, Lady Wyndham," Marian told her.

"I am very grateful," the woman retorted bluntly. "You did my Amelia a great favor when you took her in hand. Besides. Knew your father. He was a good man. I've always thought it wasn't entirely his fault he died penniless. Something havey-cavey about that solicitor he had. And so I've always said."

She paused, thumped her cane, and said, "Come along. I've some people I want you to meet. Can't expect me to help you unless you make a push to help yourselves."

From across the room, Lady Merriweather watched her nephew and that woman and Lady Wyndham. Why on earth was she smiling and talking to Miss Tibbles as if she approved of her?

She glanced the other way. There was Cunnington. He was supposed to entrance Miss Tibbles. Lure her away from Andrew. Why wasn't he doing so?

Lady Merriweather moved with a purpose and soon Mr. Cunnington found himself in a corner with her.

"What is going on?" Cordelia hissed. "You were supposed to attach yourself to Miss Tibbles!"

Cunnington shrugged. "I did so. And then your nephew joined us and it became clear that I ought to retreat. One cannot," he said sardonically, "press the romantic point when one is being threatened with bodily harm."

Lady Merriweather fanned herself faster. "Yes, yes," she said impatiently, "but what are you going to do about it? You must succeed in engaging her attention and then her affections. Before my nephew marries the woman!"

Cunnington smiled thinly. "I shall do so, never doubt it. But carefully. Miss Tibbles is no silly young chit. I shall contrive to encounter her tomorrow, as if by accident, and further my acquaintance with her. I shall be very much surprised if she is not hanging on to me by this time next week, instead of your nephew."

Cordelia nodded approvingly. "Very good. That would certainly do the trick. I cannot imagine my nephew marrying a woman who played him false."

Cunnington started to speak, then changed his mind. He merely bowed and moved away. Far be it for him to disillusion a lady prepared to pay him a tidy sum to help bring about her dearest fantasy. No more than Lady Merriweather could he truly imagine that he might fail.

Chapter 16

Marian awoke the next morning with the sense that all was remarkably well with the world. To be sure, there were those who had snubbed her at Lady Merriweather's event. But others had been kind. Perhaps it was not so foolish to contemplate marrying Andrew, after all. If she could discover the truth about him, that is.

As always, when she was distracted, Miss Tibbles chose to go for a walk. She found herself near Hatchard's and stepped into the elegantly appointed bookstore. One or two other early visitors nodded to her, while a third sniffed disdainfully and turned away. Marian suppressed a tiny sigh. Would it always be so?

Even as she reached for a book, someone bumped into her from behind. Immediately there were profuse apologies.

"I beg your pardon, ma'am! I am so profoundly sorry! It was my fault entirely!"

Marian turned to give the gentleman something of a setdown. But she didn't. He was regarding her with too much good humor in his eyes, inviting her to laugh at his clumsiness. And she almost did.

He took advantage of her momentary silence to exclaim, "Miss Tibbles! Now I am doubly sorry for my clumsiness. I would not, for the world, be in your bad graces!"

A smile tugged at the corners of her mouth. He was an

engaging creature. "There is no harm done, Mr. Cunnington," she said briskly.

"Ah, but there is," he said, placing a hand over his heart. "Harm to my poor self-image for I am wont to think of myself as a rather handsome and graceful figure and I cannot claim so if I am bumbling about, stumbling against others, particularly ladies."

Marian tilted her head to one side. She still smiled, but suddenly she found herself on guard. There was something just a trifle odd about Mr. Cunnington. Behind his amusing nonsense, she had the strangest notion that he was watching her reactions rather carefully.

Perhaps it was no more than a fellow anxious to be certain he has not given unpardonable offense. But Miss Tibbles had long ago learned to look for that which others tried to conceal and she thought she saw a hint of something here. So now she murmured something unintelligible and waited to see what Mr. Cunnington would say next.

"Have you found anything to read?" he asked politely.

Marian showed him the book she was holding, he made one of two remarks about its popularity, she asked him if he was here looking for something for himself or carrying out a request for someone else. He admitted he was executing a command on behalf of his neighbor, an intimidating dowager whose health did not permit her to come to Hatchard's herself.

The conversation ought to have died a natural death. Mr. Cunnington ought to have taken his leave of Miss Tibbles. He did not. She had the oddest notion he had something he had not yet brought himself to the point of saying. Unfortunately, they were beginning to draw the attention of others in the bookshop.

Perhaps that was why Marian felt such relief when she saw Andrew enter Hatchard's and come straight toward them.

"Good morning, Miss Tibbles," he said with a warm smile to her. Then, a trifle frostily, "Morning, Cunnington."

Cunnington bowed in return. "Good morning, Merriweather," he answered, completely undaunted. "I was just speaking to Miss Tibbles. She is a remarkable lady, you know. I was about to invite her to take a turn in the park with me, but now that you are here I am certain she would prefer your company to mine."

"Yes, I am certain she would," Andrew agreed, through clenched teeth.

Marian raised her eyebrows. She considered objecting. It was not part of her nature to allow others to make decisions or speak for her. But something held her silent.

Mr. Cunnington turned toward her and bowed yet once again. "Who knows," he said lightly, "perhaps we shall encounter one another here tomorrow."

"I think not!" Andrew said, like a shot. "Tomorrow Miss Tibbles and I are going on a picnic."

Marian's eyebrows rose even higher. Now this was too much! Andrew had become much too high-handed if he thought he could dispose of her time without even asking her wishes.

Before she could speak, however, someone else did so. A nearby matron turned to the small group and said, her voice filled with icy disdain, "If you wish to make the entire bookshop a present of your intentions, gentlemen, that is, of course, your affair. I cannot think, however, that any lady could countenance such indiscretion with anything like complacency."

"I do not," Marian instantly agreed.

Mr. Cunnington and Andrew both immediately began to apologize and excuse their having done so. The matron, however, was not done.

She looked Marian up and down and then said, witheringly, to Andrew, "I doubt very much that this lady's reputation could stand going on a picnic with you, sir. Not unless you mean to make it a group affair."

"I shall be happy to come along," Mr. Cunnington said promptly.

Andrew ignored him and turned to her, a stricken look in his eyes as he said, "Marian! That is, Miss Tibbles, I hadn't thought."

But this was too much for her. Before he could say anything more, Marian, her temper rising, turned to the matron and said, in a voice which had been known to reduce employers practically to tears upon occasion, "I thank you for your concern but it is quite misplaced. I, of all people, know what constitutes propriety! Neither I nor Colonel Merriweather require any lectures on the subject."

Then, before the matron could say anything more, she set her book back on the shelf and began to march toward the door. Over her shoulder she said to the matron, "I shall go on a picnic, if I wish. And no small-minded pettiness shall stop me!"

Once out on the street, Marian discovered that Andrew had followed her, but not Mr. Cunnington. She ought to regret her hasty words, flung so defiantly at the matron, but she could not. Particularly not when Andrew was looking at her with such a mixture of both approval and concern in his eyes. Still, Marian did feel herself blush.

From his vantage point across the street, to which he had hastily retreated when he saw Miss Tibbles heading toward the door of the bookshop, Mr. Wilkerson watched. He didn't know what had sent the woman into a rage, but he could see that she was. Interesting. Most interesting.

Another man emerged from Hatchard's. The gent what Miss Tibbles were talking to inside. He looked familiar to Wilkerson, though the Runner could not say why. But it would come to him, he was certain it would.

Meanwhile, his concern was Miss Tibbles and Colonel Merriweather. Hadn't the woman any sense at all? How could she keep spending time with a man like that? Wilkerson felt a sharp sense of exasperation that his hard work was being ignored, that she wouldn't listen to his best efforts to warn her away.

The Bow Street Runner shook his head. He wouldn't never understand women. Not in a million years he wouldn't. The other man addressed a word or two to Miss Tibbles and the colonel. Something about her stance made the Bow Street Runner look at the man a little closer.

Now, strictly speaking, other men weren't Wilkerson's problem or responsibility. He'd been hired to investigate Colonel Merriweather. But he had a shrewd notion that if Miss Tibbles were thinking of taking up with this other gent, his employer would be right happy to know about it. And about the gent.

There was something, though the Runner couldn't have said just what, about the way the gent looked at Miss Tibbles that warned he were interested in her. It worried Wilkerson, it did. He knew that sort of look, he did, and it always meant trouble. If he had a moment, Wilkerson rather thought he'd see what he could find out. He had a notion, he did, that it would pay off right well.

But meanwhile there were the colonel and Miss Tibbles to follow. They was heading toward the park and he'd head the same way. Weren't no one could say it were a crime to share the same path now was there?

Mind you, he'd give a great deal to be able to be close enough to overhear the colonel and Miss Tibbles. Probably filling her head with nonsense, Wilkerson thought with a snort of disgust. Why else would the woman be foolish enough to walk with him after what he'd taken such pains to let her know about the man?

*   *   *

"I am not certain I like the notion of Cunnington speaking to you so freely," Merriweather told Miss Tibbles with a frown, as they moved away from Hatchard's.

She bristled. He smiled down at her and said, "There is something I cannot quite like about the man. Yes, yes, I know you will chalk it up to jealousy but I swear it is more than that. The man has a reputation of being something of a fortune hunter."

Marian did not at once speak. When she did, there was an odd note to her voice. "Do you think, then, that I ought to govern my actions, my speech by what is gossiped about those around me?" she asked.

He colored up. "I was thinking aloud. And even so, I only meant that perhaps some caution would be in order. Surely that doesn't seem so much for me to ask?"

Again she hesitated. Finally she looked up at him, a troubled look in her eyes. "No? What if it were you? And I were being told that you were a fortune hunter and I ought to be wary of you?"

Again he colored. And gave a short, sharp laugh. "Well, that is different, of course!"

She merely stared at him and, after a moment, he said, "Very well, you have made your point. But mind, I mean to ask a few questions about Mr. Cunnington."

Marian did not reply. She, too, had her suspicions about Mr. Cunnington. But she saw no need to investigate the man. After all, she was in no danger of losing her heart to *him*! The only man who posed that threat to her was walking beside her and she had already put her inquiries into train concerning him.

Still, she did not object if he asked about Mr. Cunnington. Curiosity was one of Marian's besetting sins and if Andrew could satisfy it, concerning the man, why then she would be pleased to know what he could discover.

Chapter 17

What on earth had possessed her to agree to a picnic? Marian asked herself. To be sure, it was a sunny day, surprisingly pleasant for this time of year, and anyone would be pleased to be driven up the hillside to where one could see all of Bath laid out before one.

It was also undeniably imprudent. Her wretched temper! How could she have taken up the gauntlet as she had, no matter who had thrown it down?

Still, she was here and, being a practical woman, Marian decided it would be foolish not to allow herself to enjoy the outing. She was dressed warmly, with a new bonnet she had allowed herself to splurge for, now that she knew of her inheritance, and a warm cloak. The reticule and gloves were new as well.

She was conscious of looking well, and there was a part of Miss Tibbles that exulted in slipping the almost stultifying bonds of Bath, where her every move might be watched and gossiped over by those tabbies who had nothing better to do with their days.

Here she could laugh as much as she wished and not worry that someone would say it was unbecoming in a governess. Here she could indulge to her heart's desire the joy she felt in riding beside a man who made her feel younger than she had in years.

*   *   *

Andrew had no notion why Marian was in such excellent spirits today, he merely was grateful for the happy circumstance. He set himself to raise her spirits even more, imitating some of Bath's most notorious citizens until she was laughing outright.

There was a bloom in her cheeks and a sparkle in her eyes that made his breath catch in his throat. A way she had of looking at him that made him almost lose control of the pair he was driving. Which was a remarkable feat considering that none of the nags stabled for hire in Bath could be considered anything but the most laggard of cattle!

Finally he found the spot he had scouted out several days before, in hopes that he would be able to persuade Marian to come for a drive with him. He pulled up the carriage and hobbled the horses. Then he lifted her down. He lifted down as well a blanket and basket filled with food from his aunt's cook. The woman had winked at him as she handed him the provisions so that Andrew felt as though he had at least one ally in his aunt's household.

As he laid out the blanket, Marian gazed out over Bath, for the entire city was open to their view, standing as they were on a hillside overlooking the place. The sight seemed to affect her as profoundly as it had affected him when he came this way before.

"It seems so tiny, from up here," she said. "And so oddly rigid in the way it has been laid out."

"Planning," he replied, coming up behind her and putting his hands on her shoulders.

He half expected her to object. Instead, she looked up and smiled at him and Andrew drew in his breath to keep from kissing her.

"I thought you would like it," he said, to distract the both of them.

She looked back at the city and her voice came to him over her shoulder. "I do. It is just that it seems so much larger when one is down in the streets. From up here one wonders why it should ever overwhelm one."

"Does it?" he asked softly. "I never knew you felt that way."

He could feel her frown, though her back was still to him. He dared to let his hands move from her shoulders down to her waist. Still she did not pull away. Indeed, she leaned back against him.

Her voice was thoughtful as she said, "It is not precisely the city that overwhelms one, but rather the oppressive sense of respectability. The knowledge that there are those watching one's every move and ready to censure if one does not meet the highest standards of propriety. One has moments"—and here he could hear the mischief in her voice as Marian said, "when one wants to do something utterly shocking just to rattle their absolute certainty of what is right and wrong."

Now she did pull away from him, but it was to turn around and face him. The merriment he had guessed at was evident in her expression.

"Is that why you came out with me, today?" he teased. "Because you wanted to set the cat among the pigeons?"

She hesitated, then shook her head. Marian still smiled, but there was a hint of a shadow in her eyes as she said, "No. At least, not entirely. I came because I wanted to be here with you. I know that saying so puts me beyond the pale, but I cannot bear to play such games. We are surely beyond the age of such foolishness."

Andrew felt a twinge of guilt. It was not, precisely, that he was playing games with Miss Tibbles, but there were things he had not told her. Things he did not mean to tell her until they were safely wed. If then.

Would she be angry when she learned he knew of her inheritance? Perhaps. But she must understand that it was his place to decide what was right or wrong for the both of them. It was hers to be cherished. Or something of the sort, at any rate.

Perhaps he was silent too long. He realized that Marian was regarding him quizzically. "Woolgathering?" she asked gently. "Or something far more serious?"

He shook his head, as if to clear it. "No, no," he said heartily, gallantly, "merely dazed by your beauty."

"Fustian!" she snorted. "Spanish coin! You know you need not be so nonsensical with me."

"But suppose I wish to be?" he countered playfully. "Am I not allowed to flatter you? To make you feel beautiful? To tell you how dear you are to my heart?"

Her color came and went, so quickly he almost missed it. But he could not miss the way her eyes deepened, the way she caught her bottom lip between her teeth. As though she wanted to hear his nonsense, as she called it, almost as much as she wanted to reprove him for it. Andrew took that as a very good sign!

Now he took her elbow and steered her toward the blanket. "It will be warmer over here," he said. "These bushes will shield us from the wind. And the sun is shining. It should warm us up nicely. I hope you are hungry, for my aunt's cook appears to have given us provisions sufficient for a dozen people!"

Marian did not object and Andrew congratulated himself on his handling of her. There had been times, since he found her here in Bath, when she seemed so prickly he doubted his ability to hold his own irritation in check. But today she was all amiability. As a woman should be. No doubt he had mistaken a natural reserve on her part for an unbecoming desire to set her will in opposition to his.

For someone who had commanded large numbers of men, and even once been married, Colonel Merriweather was, it appeared, capable of completely misreading someone's character. But perhaps it was merely a natural desire to have the lady of his choice seem to conform to his ideal.

Marian wondered at her complacency herself. Certainly no one who knew her well and who saw her here in Bath, whenever she was in the company of Colonel Merriweather, would have believed their eyes and ears.

Even she did not entirely believe it. Or approve. Indeed, in her heart, she knew that this was what most kept her from agreeing to marry the colonel.

It frightened her that he could have such an effect upon her. That she, who was accustomed to commanding not only the girls in her charge but, when necessary, entire households, should defer so easily to what he wished. It worried her, that if she married Andrew, she might lose herself, she might lose the very core of being that made her who she was.

Which meant, she thought wryly, that she sounded just like Penelope. She tried to give herself the same advice she had once given the Earl of Westcott's youngest daughter. But somehow she did not find it in the least comforting. Perhaps because she found the advice no easier to believe than Penelope had.

Marian sighed inwardly. She wished she could make up her mind. She had told Andrew that she could not marry him because of the difference in their circumstances, but she knew in her heart that had she not had these other fears, those differences would not have weighed heavily enough to prevent her from doing what she wished.

Perhaps that was what made her so determined to be kind to him today, to try to relax in his company and let go of her fear. She did not truly wish to spend the rest of her life a spinster, if there was no need to do so.

Andrew was right. In the spot where he had laid out the blanket and set down the basket, it was warmer. As he drew out plates and utensils and food and wine, Marian settled on the opposite corner of the blanket.

But he would have none of it. As soon as everything was laid out, he moved to sit beside her. And insisted on feeding her the choicest tidbits himself.

Soon they were both laughing and, looking up at Andrew, Marian knew that this was a man she could love. That this was a man she already did love.

The thought made her breath catch in her throat and the smile slip away from her face. She even, though she was not conscious of doing so, drew back from him.

Instantly Andrew set down his plate. As if from a distance, she heard him say, "Marian? Miss Tibbles? Are you all right? Is something wrong?"

She shook her head. She tried to speak lightly but even she could hear the constraint evident in her voice.

"No. I, that is, it is nothing. Just a moment's chill, that is all."

He was all solicitude. He took her plate away from her and set it down beside his own. Then he drew her onto his lap and held her close, as though to warm her.

And the trouble was, it did, but not, surely, in the manner in which he intended to do so. She meant to hold stiff, but found herself instead, she could not have said how, leaning against his chest, her head tucked snugly under his chin, her bonnet on the ground beside her.

Miss Tibbles knew she ought to object. But Marian could not. Not when it felt so good, so right, to be here. She even, she noted with a detached sense of horror, clutched his coat with her fingers.

Gently he detached those fingers and kissed them, one by one. And still she did not object. He tilted up her chin and before she knew what he meant to do, he bent his head close to hers and gently kissed her.

At least it was meant to be a gentle kiss. Marian would have staked her life on that. But it didn't remain a gentle kiss. She heard a muffled curse, though she could not have said whether it came from her throat or his, and then the kiss deepened.

Her fingers were once again clutching the lapels of his coat. And her body arched itself against him as a moan unmistakably escaped her own lips.

This was not what she planned. This was not, her head told her, what she wanted. But it was what she did. And when the tip of his tongue hesitantly touched her lips, she parted them willingly.

How long had it been since a man kissed her? Too long. Years. Decades. Not counting the men who had tried to force kisses on her, of course. Those didn't count. No, it had been almost twenty years since Marian had wanted any gentleman to kiss her, since she had kissed any back.

And even then, a part of her recalled, they had all been chaste salutes compared to this! Nor would the girl she had been ever have allowed a gentleman's hands to wander as Andrew's were wandering now.

That alone should have shocked her into stopping. And it did. But not nearly as swiftly as it should have done. Not nearly as swiftly as the prim and proper Miss Tibbles would have demanded, had she been in charge.

But it was Marian who had to find the strength to pull away. It was Marian who had to somehow put a stop to what was going on between them. And she did. But it was with a reluctance that she could not, and perhaps did not want to, hide from Andrew.

His breathing was as ragged as her own and he rested his forehead against hers. "Forgive me," he said, his voice an odd shadow of itself. "I ought to be horse-whipped for treating you this way!"

Even as he spoke, he set her aside and scrambled to his feet. He moved to stand by the far corner of the blanket, as if he could not trust himself to come any closer. He held himself stiffly, his face etched with lines of dismay that must, she thought, match her own. Save, perhaps that it was worse in his case. Marian knew, without his saying so, that Andrew blamed himself. And that was something she could not bear.

She slowly, gracefully rose to her feet, her bonnet ignored where he had set it down sometime before. She took a step toward him, amazed at how hard it was to set one foot steadily ahead of the other. How hard not to run to Andrew, even now.

Marian placed a hand on his arm, unable to form the words she knew she ought to say. He placed his over it, as though grateful for what she meant.

"We ought to go back," he said, almost harshly.

She nodded. He forced himself to go on.

"I didn't mean for this to happen, Marian. It was never my intent to treat you with such disrespect."

Despite herself, she smiled. And gently, foolishly teased him. "Was it disrespect? I would have given it another name, myself."

He flinched. "You are not yourself, Marian. Or perhaps you are simply too innocent to realize how imprudent this has been. Well, I cannot wonder at it. I shall have to have a care for both of us. Come, we had best go back to Bath right now."

And they did. Marian did not try to dissuade him for his face made it plain she could not possibly succeed. They were an amazingly silent pair until Marian wanted to take Andrew by the shoulders and shake him.

It was not that she was pleased by their improper behavior. But to act as if a major tragedy had occurred was not something she could abide with patience! She believed in facing reality straight on and in this case she would have far preferred a calm discussion of the event.

But perhaps, she consoled herself, he had been so strongly affected he could not be calm and if that were so, then at least she was not at a disadvantage here. For certainly her own thoughts were disordered, her own emotions thrown into turmoil by what had passed between them. It was, in some ways, encouraging to know he had felt the same.

He was foolish to blame himself so deeply, but then Miss Tibbles had often observed that men were foolish. And it meant that he needed her all the more. She would have been a very strange woman indeed if she had not found that thought reassuring to contemplate!

Chapter 18

Back in Bath, Colonel Merriweather returned Miss Tibbles to her lodgings. He spoke stiffly and by the time he left her there, had not unbent in the slightest.

Aware of the interested regard of her landlady, Marian was powerless to call him to task for it. All she could do was formally thank him for the outing.

And just as formally he assured her that it had been his pleasure. Though that made him color up and Marian thought, with some exasperation, nothing could more surely signal to anyone watching, including Mrs. Stonewell, that more had passed between them than ought to have done.

So it was, therefore, something of a relief to reach her room. She paused only long enough to collect her mail on the way upstairs.

There were more letters from the various Westcott girls and Marian was strongly tempted to consign them to the fireplace unopened. But that would not do, of course and so, with a sigh, she sat down to read them as well as the rest of her mail.

Rebecca and Hugh, at least showed some sense. While disturbed by the reports the Runner had sent them, Hugh also pointed out that the colonel had an excellent reputation, in the military. Rebecca did worry that that same reputation called him autocratic and she feared he and her dear Miss Tibbles might find themselves at loggerheads for, try as she might, she could not imagine her dear governess meek and compliant!

That made Marian smile. She reached for another of the letters. Diana was exhorting her to bring the colonel up to scratch as soon as possible. Annabelle once more begged her to come and stay with them. Barbara wrote that it pained her more than she could say to know that her dearest Miss Tibbles was making a cake of herself in Bath.

Marian snorted in a most unladylike way. If anyone were to talk of scandalous behavior, it ought not to be Barbara! How glad she was not to have care of that girl any longer. Barbara was a dear girl, but she had caused Miss Tibbles a great deal of worry in her turn.

Marian saved Penelope's letter for last. She was afraid that it would once again urge her to come to London and claim her inheritance and disappear from Colonel Merriweather's sight. But she could not do it.

Nor, she decided, could she answer these letters today. She had no patience for any of their nonsense. Particularly not after what had happened between herself and Andrew up on the hillside. Instead she turned to the rest of her mail. Ah, here were letters from several of her former charges. Perhaps one of them knew something about Andrew. And they did. But it was the same mix of gossip and speculation and opinion that she had already heard from the Westcott girls.

Marian sighed. In the end, she supposed she would have to simply trust her own instincts. They told her to trust Andrew and yet there were undoubtedly reasons to wonder.

But she didn't want to think about those reasons now. Marian wanted to savor the memory, the sensations, of what had happened up there on the hillside today.

She was no green girl, so ignorant of life and what went on between men and women, that she could not

guess where matters might have led. She knew something
of the mechanics, having caught at least one of her
charges over the years in *flagrante delicto*. Not, she was
thankful to say, one of the Westcott girls!

Still, Marian was sufficiently ignorant to wonder what
it must feel like, for it had looked very strange. She could
not help being curious as to whether it could feel as wonderful as Andrew's embrace today. It must, surely, for
why else would anyone do it?

The very thoughts she was having caused Marian to
blush a fiery red, even though she was alone in her room.
And yet she was also curiously defiant. As she must have
been, a little more than twenty years earlier when her parents caught her kissing Freddy Carrington in the hedges.

Odd how she'd forgotten that. How she'd pushed away
the memory, all these years. Perhaps it was because she
always felt that it was due to her parents catching them
that his father had purchased him a set of colors.

Well, at least no one knew of today's embrace and
there were no angry parents to ring a peal over her head
this time, she thought with a fond smile. At least this im-
propriety would stay strictly between themselves.

There were occasions when Miss Tibbles was far too
optimistic. This was one of them. She had forgotten about
the Bow Street Runner.

Wilkerson was in a quandary. He'd been hired to find
out about this Colonel Merriweather fellow, but he'd also
been hired to make sure the governess lady stayed safe.
Which he'd been trying to do. But she didn't make it
easy. She didn't make it easy, at all. 'Twixt the colonel
and this new fellow, a Mr. Cunnington as he were called,
Wilkerson didn't know what to think.

He'd wager Miss Tibbles hadn't even read the report
he gave her. Or considered, properlike, what he'd had to
say about the colonel's first wife.

Come to think on it, there weren't nothing proper about the way she'd behaved, up on the hillside, that he could see at all. But were that his affair? And were he supposed to tell Mr. Rowland in his next report? But if he did, would the gentleman blame him for not interfering?

Quality! the Runner thought bitterly. Asks you to do the impossible and blames you no matter how hards you tries. He ought, he decided, to include something that would make it clear the lady weren't taking his information seriously. But he needn't tell Mr. Rowland all what he had seen. He weren't handing his head to anyone for washing, no thank you, he weren't!

Still and all, he'd feel better if he had something more solid on the colonel to send as well. But he hadn't found out anything. At least nothing to the colonel's discredit and by now the Runner was loath to include anything that wasn't. Seemed as if he'd decided to act right proper so long as he stayed with his aunt.

Except when he were up on a hillside with Miss Tibbles where he thought there weren't no one to see. Well, he was mistaken. And mayhap there were other times when the colonel thought no one were watching, here in town, and he were likewise careless here.

That thought cheered up the Runner immeasurably and he picked up his pace a bit as he followed the colonel down the street.

Andrew was completely unaware of the Runner following him. He was too preoccupied with what had happened today on the hillside over Bath. Not for the world would he have distressed Marian. And he knew she had a right to be. However strong his emotions toward her, it was his responsibility to keep them in check until their wedding night. And even beyond. So his mother had told him.

Even as he thought tibbes things, Andrew felt a tiny

quiver of joy in his heart. He knew that a wife was supposed to be treated with respect, and he meant to do so with Marian. But he also could not help rejoicing at the hint of passion in her nature. Passion she had obviously kept well hidden all these years.

There had been a charming innocence about her even as she met his kiss with one as passionate as his own. But it meant that he could hope his marriage might have more warmth to it than his first marriage had had. He would have vowed to be faithful, under any circumstances, for his sense of honor would not allow otherwise, but he could be glad that temptation would not be strong. Not when this time, he had a wife at home able to desire him as he desired her.

People passing the colonel were startled that he seemed to give them the cut direct, until they noticed the curious smile that played about his mouth and they told one another, dryly, that the colonel was evidently a man deeply in love. No doubt the governess everyone said he'd lost his senses over. Such a delicious scandal that was!

But the smile was about more than being in love with Marian. It was about his plans for her, on their wedding night. Not his plans for their wedding bed, though his mind touched on that as well, but his plans to present her with the news of her inheritance and the papers that would forever leave control of its funds in her own hands.

It was a shocking thing to contemplate and any man of his acquaintance would not hesitate to call him a fool. But Andrew had thought long and hard about this. And he smiled as he anticipated Marian's expression when he gave her this proof of how much he cared about her and about her happiness.

Andrew frowned. Ought he to wait so long to tell her about her inheritance? Would it make a difference to how she felt about him?

No, of course not, he told himself stoutly. And she did not seem to be in any difficulty for lack of funds. If she had been, of course it would have been different. But her lodgings were paid for and she was not, at the moment, seeking a new post. No, he would go ahead with his plans and surprise her on their wedding night. For he had no doubt that, sooner or later, he would overcome all her scruples and Marian would become his wife.

So intent was he on his thoughts, that Andrew might never have noticed the fellow following him if he hadn't crashed straight into him when he stopped suddenly.

Immediately, instinctively, the colonel whirled around and grabbed his assailant before the fellow could hare off. The man was startled, then he cringed, trying to pull free. Andrew refused to let him go.

"Pickpocket are you?" he demanded in the thundering tone his troops would have recognized only too well.

The man shook his head.

"A thief, then? Escaping with some merchant's goods perhaps?"

Again the man shook his head. It was at that moment Andrew realized the fellow looked familiar. Slowly he eased his grip just a little. He allowed the man to feel a touch of relief. And then, with a voice dangerously soft he delivered the fatal blow.

"Who are you and why do you keep following me?"

"Oi were one of yer soldiers oi were," the fellow whined in a pitiful voice. "Oi were 'oping yer would give me a bit of 'elp loike, oi did."

Was it possible? Andrew did not recognize the fellow, but then there had been many men who served under him and he could not know them all by sight. And this was not, after all, the first time such a thing had happened to him. So, grumbling slightly, he pulled out a handful of coins and thrust them at the fellow, who grabbed them gratefully.

"Thank yer, Colonel. Thanks yer very much."

Then, before Andrew could think to ask his name, the fellow took off. Which was perhaps just as well. He could now go back to thinking about Marian.

Except, there had been something odd about the fellow, Andrew realized as he strode down the sidewalk, a little more careful than before. He could not have said just what it was that troubled him.

Finally he shrugged. What difference did it make? He had both his purse and his watch so if the man had been after thievery, he had accomplished nothing.

No, far more likely, one way or another, the fellow was a beggar and settled on him as an easy mark. Well, now the fellow was gone and good riddance. He would not have the nerve to approach Andrew twice so one might as well forget the fellow.

Abruptly Andrew decided to turn into a nearby shop and have some flowers delivered to Marian. It would both wipe the taste of the encounter with the stranger out of his mouth and serve as an apology to her.

He never realized that the man he dismissed so lightly still followed, albeit at a greater, more cautious distance now.

Chapter 19

Colonel Merriweather might have forgotten about the man who had been following him if he had not seen him again so soon. And in such disturbing circumstances.

Andrew arrived at Miss Tibbles' lodgings the next day just a little too late to catch her. He decided to follow in the direction the landlady had indicated and he walked briskly, impatient to see the woman he loved.

To his profound shock, he saw the same man, who had crashed into him the day before, following Marian. He saw her stop and speak to him and then try to rush away. The fellow seemed to protest for Marian shook her head, distress evident in every line of her body.

Andrew felt an overpowering sense of rage. Even as he moved faster toward them, he saw Marian escape into a shop and the fellow turn and come toward him. The fellow's head was down and he did not see the colonel. Otherwise he would surely never have made such a fatal error as that!

A moment later, Andrew had the astonished man by the collar of his coat. With a swift look around, the colonel realized he could not interrogate him here. He hauled him down a narrow alleyway and the fellow was too shaken to protest. There, out of sight of the gentry taking the air, Andrew thrust the man against a wall.

"What the devil were you doing following that lady?" he demanded.

" 'oping fer a 'andout," the fellow said, in a wheedling tone.

"I think not," Andrew said curtly. "I watched the entire exchange."

It was Andrew's turn to be astonished as the fellow seemed to change before his very eyes. His accent altered and he said, in a sullen voice, "I meant the lady no harm."

"Who are you? And don't try to tell me a former soldier for I shan't believe you!"

The man sighed. He pulled himself free from Colonel Merriweather's grip and straightened his coat. "I'm a Bow Street Runner, I am," he said, tilting up his chin defiantly. "On His Majesty's business and I'll thank you, sir, not to interfere."

"A Bow Street Runner?" Andrew echoed, his jaw hanging open in disbelief. "But why would you wish to speak with Miss Tibbles?"

"That, sir, is between me and her."

Andrew blustered, but it was to no avail. The man would tell him nothing. And in the end he had to let him go, for interfering with a Bow Street Runner was not something one did lightly.

It never occurred to Andrew to wonder why the man had been following him. All his concern was for Marian and why a Runner should be following her!

Even as he slowly retraced his steps he turned that question over and over in his mind. The only thing he could think of, the only thing that even made the slightest sense was that someone thought perhaps she had stolen something from them. It was absurd, of course. Undoubtedly a mistake. Nonetheless it could only be distressing to Marian to have a Runner following her about.

The very least he could do was to reassure her that he had sent the fellow to the rightabout.

Except that he hadn't. The fellow might well plan to continue to follow her.

Why, Andrew wondered, was he so determined to do so? Surely anyone looking at Marian would know she could not possibly be a thief. Unless, perhaps, there were some sort of evidence to prove that she was?

Slowly, Andrew could not have said when, he began to entertain the possibility that Miss Tibbles had committed some sort of indiscretion. His father had had a cousin, he suddenly remembered, who was unable to resist taking little things, whenever she stayed in someone else's house. Her friends all knew it and her husband had always quietly returned what was missing and so no one had ever called the Runners down upon her head for it. Perhaps Marian suffered from such a compulsion as well.

And after all, it was hard to imagine the Runners sending someone after her unless they had good reason to suppose she had done something.

The devil was, how was he to find out? He could not simply ask Marian if she had taken things! Even if it was true, then like his father's cousin, she would almost certainly deny having done so.

The other possibility that occurred to him, scarcely on the heels of the first, was that Marian was the target of some villain. Perhaps some angry past employer. Perhaps some gentleman whom she would not allow to take liberties with her. Perhaps a former charge who wished to make trouble for her now.

Andrew didn't know. He only knew that whichever explanation was the correct one, he would stand by Marian and protect her. He would not allow anyone to harm her. Nor allow her to harm herself.

The first thing, he decided, was to determine the precise nature of the threat against Miss Tibbles. To that end, he once more reversed direction and headed for her lodgings, where he intended to wait for her as long as it might take for her to return.

It might, he conceded, have been prudent to catch up

with her, instead, and accompany her as she visited the shops to make certain nothing unfortunate occurred, but Andrew was not quite ready to do so. He could, he decided, use a little time to compose himself first.

Marian was not precisely surprised to find Colonel Merriweather waiting when she returned to her lodgings, but she did find herself oddly shy in his presence. That he remembered what had occurred yesterday as clearly as she did seemed confirmed by the way he also colored up and had difficulty meeting her eyes with his own.

Perversely that caused Marian to feel a little better and she greeted him more calmly than she would have thought possible.

"Andrew! How kind of you to come to see me."

"I, er, would you care to go out for a walk with me? I know you have just returned but, I, er, it is a very fine day outside."

"So it is," Marian agreed, her eyes dancing. "Give me a moment to take my parcels upstairs and I shall be happy to go for a walk with you."

She did not keep him waiting very long. She was eager to be with him and her parcels could be unwrapped later. For now she hurriedly repinned her hair, adjusted her bonnet more becomingly, and went back downstairs.

He was in quiet conversation with the landlady, but for once Marian was not troubled by it. She had almost made up her mind to marry him and to the devil with everyone's doubts and fears and concerns. Indeed, she could understand wanting to know all one could. And he came away the instant he saw Marian on the stairs.

Still, there seemed an odd constraint about the colonel as he held the door for her. And once they started walking he seemed to be asking the oddest questions.

"You must have had some unusual experiences while you were a governess," he began.

Marian was just a little puzzled. "Well, yes, I did have some," she agreed. "One cannot help doing so when one is called in as a governess, as I was, to take charge of girls too outrageous for their parents to handle. But I have told you before I cannot and will not speak of any indiscretions I had to deal with."

"I, er, were there any parents who were not happy with how you dealt with their daughters?"

Marian hesitated, a tiny frown between her eyes. "I suppose there may have been, but I do not think so. To be sure, no family ever needed my services very long and none begged me to stay afterwards, but then there was no need for me once their daughters were safely married. I was of no further use to them and naturally they were perfectly willing to see me take a post elsewhere."

Andrew mopped his brow and Marian became more puzzled than ever. She had never seen him this distracted before. Still, he persisted with his odd questions.

"What about your charges?" he asked, a hint of desperation in his voice. "Did any of them hold a grudge against you? Ever accuse you of improper behavior?"

Now that was odd enough to cause Marian to stop and turn to stare at Andrew in disbelief.

"I only meant," he stammered, "that young girls can be very emotional and very foolish and I have heard of girls making trouble for their governesses."

Marian began walking again. "Well, yes, it has happened. And once to a friend of mine. She was accused of stealing some very valuable pearls. They were, fortunately, found in the daughter's keeping but my friend was still turned off without a character. For the crime of not being able to keep the girl in better check."

Marian shuddered. "I thank heavens none of the girls I cared for have ever done such a thing."

She paused. Bluntness was called for, she decided.

"What is it, Andrew? Why do you ask such odd things

of me? Do you fear some former charge of mine will try to make trouble for us? Has one of them already done so? Tried to traduce my character to you? If so, I should very much like to know who would have done such a thing. And precisely what they might have said."

"No, no, I have heard from none of your former charges," he said hastily. "Save, of course, for Westcott's daughters and you were there when they spoke to me."

Marian nodded, still not satisfied. Abruptly she realized what this might all be about! His wife. Did he fear someone had traduced him to her? And if so, what could she say to him? What would he think if he knew someone had told her he had murdered his first wife? Jest that she did not have a sufficient portion to be in any danger?

Unable to think of what to say, she was silent and waited for what he might ask. His next words seemed even stranger than before.

"When you were living in those houses—elegant mansions, most of them I should think, given the families you have told me you were governess for—were you ever envious of all the finery?"

"Often," Marian admitted ruefully. "It was my besetting sin. I kept remembering Mama's jewels and how they had had to be sold to pay off Papa's debts. And the furniture, so elegant, more elegant than even when Papa seemed most prosperous."

She paused and smiled at him. "The worst temptations were the gowns. Mama had never allowed me to have the silks and satins I wished for, telling me I was far too young. She died and Papa kept putting me off, saying I must still wait until I was older. I had no notion then that money was a problem for us. And when I was older, on my own, I could neither afford them nor would it have been proper for a governess to wear such things. And now you know the worst about me and are horridly disappointed!" she teased.

"Never!" he countered and squeezed her hand reassuringly. "And I promise you, Marian, you shall have whatever jewels and dresses and furniture you wish, once we are married. You need never envy anyone else ever again."

Marian smiled but shook her head. "I fear I shall always be subject to some degree of envy. I am merely human, you know. But I have long since learned to come to terms with the reality of my existence and I do not truly repine over any of it, I assure you."

"You are fortunate then," he said quietly, as though inviting further confidences. "Many cannot become so sanguine. Indeed, temptation can become almost overwhelming. They are not, in the end able to resist. And sometimes I blame most those who put temptation in their way."

Marian frowned. She had the sense Andrew was trying very hard to tell her something and she feared she knew what it must be. If so, she did not wish to hear it. And yet, if he had murdered his first wife, for her inheritance, could she bear herself if she ignored such a thing?

Of course not. With an inward sigh, Marian said, gently, in her most serious voice, "One might envy. Temptation might seem overwhelming. Perhaps some things I might even be able to forgive. But there must always be limits. One must never harm another."

Now he was the one who could not seem to decide how to answer and Marian felt her heart sink. Why else should he be struck so dumb unless it was because her words had cut too close to the bone?

And yet she did not wish it to be so! She had come to care deeply, perhaps too deeply, for Andrew and she wanted him to say, she wanted to hear, that all the suspicions were nonsense! She did not wish to believe that her words could rob him of any way to answer.

After a long moment he said, forcing a smile, "Yes, of

course you are right. There must be limits. I am glad to hear you draw the line at harming anyone."

It was meant to be a jest but it fell sadly flat. It would have been difficult to tell, Marian thought, which of them was more blue-deviled.

Abruptly she said, "Will you take me back to my lodgings, Colonel Merriweather? I—I have the headache and wish to lie down in the darkness of my room."

"Of course."

He was punctilious in his politeness, making no mention of, or objection to, the fact he had gone from Andrew to Colonel Merriweather in her estimation. Indeed, it seemed to Marian that he was as eager to be rid of her as she was of him. And despite everything, that distressed her.

How she could wish for the company, the attention, the affection of a man who might be a murderer was beyond her! Indeed, it was beyond any foolishness any of her charges had ever indulged in.

And yet, it was undeniably true.

Slowly Marian mounted the steps to her room, her headache very real by now. With one hand, she gripped the railing tightly. From her other hand dangled the strings of her bonnet and one more letter. This one from Lord Farrington.

Marian fought back tears as she opened the letter. All she needed was one more person haranguing her to send the colonel to the rightabout.

But that was not what Lord Farrington had to say. Instead, his letter informed her that having discovered what was going on, he wished to assure her, quite strongly, that she was not to listen to idle gossip. He wished her to know that Colonel Merriweather was a good man and that Farrington could not imagine wishing to serve with one better.

Yes, but, Marian thought as she set the letter aside, would he wish to marry him?

Still, it was encouraging. At least one person admired Andrew. If only she could find proof that all the rumors about his wife's death were groundless. Her fear was that, particularly after today, she was more likely to find they were true.

Without meaning to, her fingers reached out and picked up Lord Farrington's letter. She read it through again and carried it with her to the bed as she lay down, her headache a trifle lighter already.

Chapter 20

Mr. Wilkerson was most distressed. How could he have made such a fatal error as to draw to himself the attention of Colonel Merriweather? If this got out and the other Bow Street Runners came to hear what a feeble-witted clunch he had been, they would never stop roasting him!

Still, he would have to report something. Otherwise, if anyone came to hear of what had passed between them, because Colonel Merriweather said something about the incident, the trouble would be ten times worse.

It was all the colonel's fault, of course. He oughtn't to have been so suspiciouslike. It weren't normal, it weren't. It just proved, didn't it, that the colonel had a guilty conscience and were just waiting for someone to catch him. Well, didn't it?

Mr. Wilkerson conveniently allowed himself to forget that Colonel Merriweather had accosted him when he was following Miss Tibbles. Or that anyone might have thought it odd to see a character such as himself speak to someone like her. Instead he nursed his grudge against the colonel until it loomed even larger than before.

Never, in all his times as a Runner, had anyone humiliated him as the colonel had. At least, he told himself with some pride, he hadn't let on to the colonel that he weren't following the lady but rather reporting to her about the colonel. He wouldn't want to be the one to place her in danger, he wouldn't, if the colonel was to discover she were hearing about his past.

And he might, too. Everything he saw and heard seemed to prove the colonel were bent on marrying Miss Tibbles and getting his fingers on her money. Well, Mr. Wilkerson weren't about to stand by and let it happen. Not if he could do anything about the matter.

By now the Runner was beyond the point of being able to be objective about things. All he knew was that he didn't like the colonel. He didn't like him at all. And he thought he knew what he ought to do.

Wilkerson went back to his rooms, once he saw that Miss Tibbles was safely back at her lodgings, alone, and the colonel no doubt headed to his aunt's house. There he found the information he had sent for concerning Mr. Cunnington.

With a grim smile, he set the information aside until he might again have the chance to speak with Miss Tibbles and warn her. Poor lady hadn't the least bit of sense when it came to men!

And this time he would make certain the colonel was nowhere about before he spoke to her. For now, he sat down and wrote his report about the encounter between himself and Colonel Merriweather.

Those who had witnessed this event might have been surprised to hear that the latter was a violent man and had assaulted the Runner without the slightest provocation. Wilkerson, however, was pleased with his prose. And no one would think, by this report, that anything which had happened could possibly be the Runner's fault. That, after all, was Wilkerson's immediate concern.

Andrew walked in a daze. It was worse, far worse, than he had thought! Marian had all but admitted she had stolen things. At least, he thought she had. To be sure, he was relieved she drew the line at hurting anyone, still it was most distressing to have his worst fears confirmed.

No wonder the Runner followed her as he did. Andrew found himself wondering just what she had stolen, from whom, and whether he could somehow make matters right.

Oh, he ought to be appalled, he knew that, and he was. But truth be told, he was more appalled by the knowledge that even so, he still cared deeply for Marian. He still wanted to protect and marry her.

Well, perhaps he was a fool, but he was old enough to know one didn't often find someone to love as he loved Marian. And it was something he could not lightly give up. Still, he warned himself, he must be prepared for rough ground ahead, for the both of them.

A moment later, it occurred to him that he had best keep as close an eye on Marian as possible and make certain she didn't steal anything while she was here in Bath. Fortunately, since she was not likely to receive social invitations from the more wealthy inhabitants of Bath, and her landlady could not possibly possess anything Marian would envy, perhaps the risk was not so very great.

A harassed look crossed Andrew's face. It was one thing to vow to love and marry the woman, despite anything. It was quite another to face the reality that entailed. He would never be able to allow her to go anywhere without him! A few days before he would have called that a delightful prospect. Today it could only fill him with dismay.

So preoccupied was he, that his appearance immediately alarmed Lady Merriweather. "Dear boy, is something the matter?" she exclaimed.

He tried to smile, he truly did. "Oh, nothing serious, Aunt Cordelia," he said lightly. "A trifling matter involving a friend."

"Miss Tibbles?" Lady Merriweather hazarded shrewdly.

He tried to shrug it off, but his face must have betrayed him.

"Oh, Andrew, you must stop courting that woman!" his aunt exclaimed impulsively.

"I cannot," he said simply.

She rose to her feet and began to pace about the room impatiently. Her exasperation was patent in her voice as she said, sharply, "This is absurd! We have spoken of it before and you refuse to listen to my sensible advice. Very well! I wash my hands of everything! I will have nothing more to do with any of this."

"So far as I can see, you have nothing to do with it now," Andrew retorted, with an attempt at humor.

Lady Merriweather was not amused. "I am quite serious, Andrew. If you mean to continue with this folly then I shall remove myself from Bath."

That truly startled Andrew. "Remove from Bath?" he echoed in a bewildered voice. "But why?"

She rounded on him. "So that your mother cannot blame me for this mésalliance you insist upon making! I will not let her lay this at my doorstep. Tomorrow I leave Bath and I am closing up the house so you shall have to find somewhere else to stay."

Now his own temper was roused. Indeed, coming so soon after the shattering encounter with the Bow Street Runner and his devastating conversation with Marian, it was more than Andrew could bear.

In a dangerously calm voice he said, "That is quite enough, Aunt Cordelia. Naturally you must do as you think best. Leave Bath, if that is your choice, but you need not do so, you know. I shall remove from this house before nightfall. Whether you stay or go, if my chosen wife is not welcome here, then neither am I."

"Andrew! I did not mean it like that!" Lady Merriweather said, reaching out a hand toward him.

"No?" He stared at her, his gaze steady. "It does not

matter. I will have no trouble finding lodgings at this time of year and I will trouble you no longer. Good-bye, Aunt Cordelia. I shall undoubtedly send you an invitation to our wedding but of course I shall not be surprised if you choose not to attend."

Then, without allowing himself to look back, Andrew left the room. He took the steps two at a time up to his room. There he rang the bell violently and the instant his batman appeared informed that hapless fellow they were leaving the house at once.

"Leaving? To go where, sir?" the batman asked, utterly confused.

"I don't know," Andrew answered ruefully. "The White Hart, if possible. If not, we shall see if York House has rooms for us."

"Then we are staying in Bath?" his batman asked, his brow wrinkled.

"Yes, of course we are staying in Bath," Andrew replied impatiently. Then, evidently feeling he must say something more, he added, "It seems Lady Merriweather has suddenly decided she wishes to remove from Bath and close up the house. I thought it best to remove ourselves as quickly as possible so she need not worry about us."

Since the batman had heard a great deal of gossip below stairs about Lady Merriweather's opinion of the colonel's interest in a certain Miss Tibbles, he had his own interpretation of this statement. Still, it was not his place to comment and he did not do so. Instead he moved to pack the colonel's belongings as swiftly as possible.

"I shall send a footman to inquire at both establishments," the batman said in a carefully expressionless voice.

"Excellent man!" Andrew said. "Whatever should I do without you?"

The batman was gratified by this, but naturally he did

not say so. Instead he continued with his work as the colonel flung himself into a chair by the window and stared out it. The batman would have wagered that however long the colonel stared, he still wouldn't see a single thing.

As soon as he was done with the packing, the batman headed for the door. "I shall send the footmen, Colonel, and pack my own things. I should think we could be ready to leave in the hour, if you wish," he said.

Andrew didn't wish it. He wished he could stay here with his favorite aunt. He wished his favorite Aunt Cordelia could be brought around to welcome Marian into the family. But that was patently not going to occur, particularly if she were to get wind of the matter, whatever it was, that had brought the Bow Street Runner to Bath in pursuit of Miss Tibbles.

Andrew shuddered at the thought. Perhaps he ought to give up Marian. Perhaps it would be a kindness to the both of them. He had already seen how the censure of others could overset her. Had he a right to marry her and subject her, subject all of them to such distress permanently?

It was a question that took Andrew very little time to decide. He remembered his wedding vows to Drusilla clearly. He had promised to care for her, for good or for ill. He could do, would do, no less for Marian. He would shield her from all the censure he could. And he would begin by removing himself from this house at once.

If his aunt was any indication of the reaction that was likely to greet the news of his betrothal, he would have to be firm with his family, letting them know at once he would not tolerate any disrespect of her.

Andrew frowned. It was odd his mother hadn't written to him about Marian. Then it occurred to him that perhaps Aunt Cordelia had not yet told her, fearing as she said, that his mother would blame her for the match.

Andrew decided that was an oversight which ought to be remedied at once. Grimly he rose from the chair. Downstairs he would find ink, pens, and paper. And the moment his batman told him to which establishment they were removing, he could add that information to his letter.

He supposed he also ought to notify his brother of his intentions. As head of the family, his brother would certainly think he ought to be informed. Andrew sighed and reached for another piece of paper.

Perhaps his mother and brother, he thought, would be kinder to Miss Tibbles than Aunt Cordelia had been.

Somehow Andrew could not bring himself to believe it.

Marian was having no easier time of it than Andrew. Her thoughts in a whirl, she had gone out again, thinking a walk in the cool air would clear her head. And the first person she encountered was Mr. Cunnington.

"Miss Tibbles!" he exclaimed, with every appearance of joy. "I was just coming to call on you."

"You were?" she echoed warily.

Undaunted he pressed on, beaming happily, "Well, you see, it is such a fine day that I thought you might enjoy a turn about the park."

He looked at her with wide, innocent eyes. Marian was immediately suspicious. No one above the age of twenty ever looked that naive and innocent unless they had some nefarious scheme in hand. She ought to refuse. Certainly Andrew would not approve.

But Marian could never resist a challenge. So instead of refusing, she took the arm Mr. Cunnington offered her, smiled up at him with the same look of innocence in her eyes as he had in his, and said sweetly, "Why, Mr. Cunnington, I should be delighted."

And if she did not have the truth about the man from

him before they were even halfway there, Marian would know she was losing her touch.

They were oh, so polite to one another. Marian asked a few questions, Mr. Cunnington evaded them neatly. He asked her a few, she was just as adept.

Finally, Marian grew impatient and decided it was time to be more direct.

"You are a friend, are you not, of Lady Merriweather?" she asked.

He hesitated. And looked down at her with a flash of alarm in his eyes. It was just for a moment, but that was enough to confirm Marian's guesses.

"I have met the lady," he said.

"Indeed?"

It was not very encouraging, but Mr. Cunnington did not yet know Miss Tibbles very well and he pressed on. "We have met on a few occasions. She was kind enough to invite me the other night."

Marian smiled thinly. "Perhaps," she said, "I ought to tell you, or rather, Lady Merriweather, that even if it were possible for me to be tempted from Colonel Merriweather's side, it would not be by a man such as you!"

He stopped. Miss Tibbles pointedly reminded him that they were making a spectacle of themselves and ought to keep walking.

He stammered. He protested. Ultimately he stopped protesting, though this time he kept walking with her, and shrugged.

"I told Lady Merriweather it would not work," he said, rather cheerfully. "I suppose I had best collect my fee before she discovers I was right."

Before Marian could reply, someone bumped into her, almost knocking her over. Even as Cunnington hurled a curse or two at the man's head, the clumsy fellow whispered urgently to her, "You oughtn't to take up with this bloke, Miss Tibbles. He ain't what he seems, y'see. Maybe you oughtn't to take up with anybody."

Slowly Marian straightened. It was, of course, the Bow Street Runner. Again. Well, enough was enough. She looked him directly in the eye and said, in a firm, clear voice, "If you do not leave me alone, I am going to make certain no one ever hires you again."

Hastily the Runner looked around with alarm, especially at Cunnington. "Here, now, no need for that. You doesn't want me to speak to you, I won't speak to you."

And then he beat a very hasty retreat.

Cunnington escorted Marian back to her lodgings, too unnerved to even ask her what that had been about. He left her there thinking that all in all, perhaps it was as well he had been unmasked. There was something distinctly unladylike and unsettling in the woman's perceptiveness and he would be perfectly happy to see her attention turned somewhere else.

Chapter 21

Miss Tibbles was completely unaware that the Runner had encountered Colonel Merriweather. She noticed that he made no further attempts to speak to her, but she was only conscious of a strong sense of relief.

She knew that perhaps she was being foolish, but if so, she wanted to be foolish! She enjoyed the days that followed, particularly now that she had disposed of Mr. Cunnington. Andrew was attentive and she spent a great deal of time in his company.

No attention was wanting as he looked after her every need. After so many years of looking after the needs of the girls in her charge, it was a very nice feeling to have someone look after her for a change. It was very nice to have an escort everywhere she went. Someone who was eager to carry her parcels for her and enter into every transaction with every shopkeeper.

It was only when Andrew pressed her to agree to marry him—and soon—that Marian felt her doubts growing stronger. There was a cynical side of her which said that even if he planned to murder her for her money, he could not do so until after they were married. She did not believe such a calumny, of course, but the more he pressed her, the more she drew back.

In the end she decided there was nothing to be done but to go to London on the stage and speak to the solicitor herself. She did not, however, intend to tell Andrew where she was going or why. Indeed, she did not intend to tell him that she would be away at all. Otherwise he might ask questions she could not answer. Or, even more likely, insist on going with her. And she was very much afraid that she, the indomitable Miss Tibbles, would not have the strength of character to refuse to allow him to do so.

She made her arrangements and it was only as she left her lodgings, bag in hand, that she said carelessly to Mrs. Stonewell, "I am going away but I shall be back in a few days. Pray keep my room for me."

Then, as the lady gaped at her in astonishment, Marian made good her escape.

At the same moment as Miss Tibbles was heading for the posting house from which the London stage would depart, six men were meeting in that very same establishment. The husbands of all five Westcott girls and the Bow Street Runner hired by Rowland.

Mr. Rowland had just arrived from the north, Lord Winsborough and the Duke of Berenford from their respective estates, and Mr. Talbot and Lord Farrington had arrived together from London. Mr. Wilkerson met them in the taproom. None of the men looked very pleased. Fortunately, someone had had the forethought to book a private parlor and they retired there quickly.

The moment they were alone, Farrington rounded on the others. "I tell you I know Colonel Merriweather and he is a good man! It is absurd to accuse him of violence or of being a threat to Miss Tibbles."

"But the report," Talbot insisted.

"Yes, the report," Rowland agreed. "Tell us, Wilkerson, precisely what occurred."

The Bow Street Runner stammered as he answered. This was not what he had envisioned when he sent off that report. It was just like the Quality, he thought bitterly, to thrust a spoke in one's plans.

"The colonel, he attacked me. Right in broad daylight, he did. I've still got the bruises to prove it. Or did, until yesterday."

"How convenient," Berenford said dryly.

"It weren't convenient, it weren't convenient at all!" Wilkerson said, incensed.

"Look, just tell us what you have found out," Winsborough replied soothingly.

Wilkerson did so, lingering on the worst suspicions he had uncovered. Indeed, he went on so long that finally Talbot said impatiently, "Yes, yes, but do you have anything which is not simply gossip? Any direct evidence to prove the things you say?"

"Well, no," he grudgingly allowed.

Farrington let out an exasperated sigh. "You see? I told you it was all nonsense!"

"Is it?" Rowland asked quietly. "What about the inheritance? Why was Colonel Merriweather in the solicitor's office, then? And why did he not tell Miss Tibbles about her inheritance?"

"Appearances can be deceiving," Winsborough temporized. "What do you think, Farrington?"

"I don't know," Farrington admitted. "But why don't we just ask Merriweather?"

"Ask me what?"

All six men had had their backs to the door and now all six started and turned to stare at Colonel Merriweather, who had opened it with none of them hearing a thing.

"How long have you been there?" Rowland asked with a frown.

Merriweather brushed a piece of lint off his sleeve and then said, coolly, "Not nearly long enough, I think." He stared at the Bow Street Runner and then at each of the other five men. His voice turned very cold. "So it is one or more of you who hired this man to follow Miss Tibbles about. I would have thought better of you."

"Better of us?" Rowland asked incredulously.

"Yes, better," Merriweather said, his mouth drawing into a thin, disapproving line. "I should have thought you would be sufficiently grateful to Miss Tibbles not to wish her any distress. Whatever you think she may have taken from you, surely it cannot be worth so much that it is not outweighed by the service she did your wives."

Five of the men in the room gaped at Colonel Merriweather. The Runner, Mr. Wilkerson, tried to sidle toward the door as if he meant to escape through it.

It was Farrington who finally spoke. "Merriweather," he said carefully, "just what is it you believe this Runner is doing in Bath?"

"I told you. Following Miss Tibbles about," Andrew retorted impatiently. "I presumed it was because someone thought she had stolen something from them. I never dreamed the Westcott family could be so ungrateful that they would pursue her like this."

Several looks were exchanged among the five men. Then they all looked at the Runner. "Just what," Berenford said in an odd voice, "did you tell Colonel Merriweather when he gave you that beating?"

"Beating?" It was Merriweather's turn to gape at them in disbelief.

Wilkerson avoided meeting anyone's eyes. Somewhat sullenly he said, "Well, I couldn't tell him I were following him, now could I? He caught me following her, meaning to tell her the latest I'd found out. I thought it were safer for her if he didn't know I'd told her what a rum 'un he was. So I let him think whatever he wished."

Merriweather gaped even more. He looked at the six men in turn, shaking his head slowly. Finally he fixed on Farrington. "I think," he said, "you had best tell me what is going on. And what you thought you ought to ask me, when I came into the room."

There was some awkwardness. Some hemming and hawing. Finally it was Winsborough who said, "The Bow Street Runner was not following Miss Tibbles, except to inform and perhaps protect her. He was sent here to discover everything he could about you. We do, you see, have a great deal of respect and affection for Miss Tibbles and we did not wish to see her taken in."

Again Merriweather fixed his gaze on Farrington, who immediately protested, "It wasn't my notion! I wasn't even asked! Had I been, I would have assured them it wasn't necessary. I was trying to tell them, right before you came in, that I know you and that you are a good man."

"But there was something you said I ought to be asked?" Merriweather persisted.

Farrington hesitated and it was Talbot who said, "Two things. We should like to ask you about your first wife's death and also ask why you visited the solicitor who holds Miss Tibbles' inheritance in his care. How did you find out about it in the first place? Oh, and why you did not tell her it was there."

Merriweather tried to smile. He failed signally. He opened his mouth to speak. And closed it again. As they watched, his shoulders sagged and he seemed to age several years.

"I cannot, I will not, speak of my wife's death," he said in a voice so low they had to strain to hear. "As for Marian's inheritance, I learned of it almost by accident. I meant to surprise her on our wedding day."

"Oh, she would have been surprised," Rowland said cynically. "Surprised to know she had a choice other than to either marry you or to take up another post as governess somewhere."

Merriweather's face hardened. "Very well," he said, "I shall tell Marian—Miss Tibbles—today."

"She already knows," Winsborough pointed out.

"I shall speak to her," the colonel said, meeting each gaze squarely, "about what I know and my reasons for keeping silent. But that is to be between her and me."

Rowland shook his head. "Oh, no. Our wives would have our heads if we left it to you like that. We must be there, to see for ourselves, that you are honest with her. And that you do not bully her into anything she does not wish to do. We must be certain."

"And if I refuse?"

As one, the five men rose and surrounded the colonel, even Farrington. He looked at his old friend and said, a wry smile on his face, "Come, Merriweather, you must know when you are beaten. I trust you, but I understand their concern. And he's quite right about our wives, you know. They have a very great fondness for Miss Tibbles. As do we all."

Merriweather did indeed know when he was beaten. He lifted an eyebrow, shrugged, turned toward the door, and said, over his shoulder, "Very well. Come along then. Quite a parade we shall make, and no doubt become the source of a great deal of conjecture. But if you are indeed so determined, I shan't bother to waste any more breath trying to turn you away from your course."

"May I go now?" the Runner asked, all but forgotten in the corner.

Rowland waved a dismissive hand. "Yes, yes. Come back later and we shall talk again. I no doubt still owe you some wages."

Wilkerson nodded but made no move toward the door. He had evidently decided to wait until they had gone before he tried to do so.

As Colonel Merriweather had said, it was an odd sight, six gentlemen moving together through the posting house and out into the yard. They were murmuring among themselves and almost didn't see the stage. But Andrew did. It was he who exclaimed, "Good heavens! What the devil is Marian doing boarding a stage for London?"

He hurried forward but already the door was shut behind her and the coachman had started the horses forward. Still, the colonel would have run after her had the others not stopped him.

"You'll cause a scene!"

They were right, of course, but he was loath to admit it. Still, it was too late. Marian was gone.

"I must go to her lodgings," he said, aloud but to himself. "Perhaps her landlady will know when she is expected back."

"If she is expected back," Talbot said.

"We shall all go," Berenford said. "At once. We are drawing too many eyes, standing here like this."

Mrs. Stonewell, however, could tell them nothing except that Miss Tibbles had said she would be back. She had not a clue as to why she had gone away and did not, she said, care to venture a guess.

Slowly, reluctantly, the men withdrew.

"Now what do we do?" Talbot asked the others, as they headed back toward the inn. "Follow the stagecoach to London? Intercept it and take her off?"

As one, the five others turned and stared at him incredulously. Very carefully Berenford said, "I should not like to face Miss Tibbles if we did so. Can you imagine what she would say to us? How impertinent she would consider our interference in her affairs? I should not care to face such a scolding. Would you?"

It was an image that caused all of them to blanch and shake their heads. All except Merriweather. "What the devil are you talking about?" he asked irritably. "Marian

is the gentlest of women! I cannot conceive of her taking
a pet and rounding on anyone."

Now it was his turn to be stared at by five incredulous
faces. Carefully, very carefully, as though he was finding
it very difficult not to laugh, Farrington looked at the
others and said, in a very serious voice, "You see? It
must be love. Either on his part or on hers. Or both.
Nothing else could possibly explain it."

Rowland stroked his chin. "You have a point," he conceded.

"Indeed, anyone who can describe Miss Tibbles as the
gentlest of women has either never seen the, shall we
say, strong side of her or else possesses extraordinary
powers of denial," Berenford agreed judiciously.

Slowly Winsborough and Talbot nodded. This was
sufficient for Merriweather to snap, "You are mad. All of
you. Utterly mad! Wanting in wits. I wonder you have
not all been clapped up in Bedlam. Good day!"

Not a one of them made the slightest effort to prevent
him from going. When he was out of sight, they looked
at one another again.

"Yes, but what are we going to tell our wives?" Talbot
was the first to put it into words.

"We shall tell them," the Duke of Berenford said
solemnly, "that the colonel is evidently a man deep in the
throes of love."

"That is all very well for you to say," Rowland grum-
bled. "Your wife is all for this marriage in the first place.
Rebecca will not be so easy to convince, I assure you.
What am I to tell her?"

"I don't know," Winsborough replied, "but what other
choice do we have? Cool our heels here in Bath until
Miss Tibbles returns?"

It was Lord Farrington who replied, "Why not? At
least it puts off the moment we must report back to our

wives as to what happened here today. And we really won't have any answers until she does."

And that, the others agreed, made wonderful sense to them. Suddenly feeling much more cheerful, they agreed to retire to the nearest pub and celebrate their reprieve.

Chapter 22

Knowledge was, Marian thought, a distinctly mixed blessing. Even as the coach pulled into Bath and she clutched her reticule, now containing an alarmingly ample amount of funds, she found herself thinking that nothing could ever be the same again.

Oh, she knew, had been told by both the Bow Street Runner and Penelope and Geoffrey, that she had an inheritance. Even the amount. But it was only when she found herself signing the documents and then accepting the first disbursal of funds into her care, that Marian fully realized the extent of the change in her circumstances.

Mind you, any of the Westcott girls would have laughed to think of it as anything more than pin money and would have been most likely to express doubt that anyone could survive on so little an amount.

But for someone to whom eighty pounds a year had been an exorbitant salary, it was a very generous portion indeed. To be sure, she would now need to pay for both her food and her own lodgings but even these would not make such great inroads on her purse. Not if she continued to practice the same level of economy she had always done.

Ah, but would she? It was tempting, so tempting to dash into the very first shop she passed and splurge on gowns and hats and gloves and reticules. But eighteen years had not been sufficient to erase the horror of discovering her father had outspent his means to the point of ruin.

Marian smiled to herself. She knew that no matter how tempting, she would not follow in his footsteps and do the same. No, she would continue to practice economy but perhaps, now, there would be, on occasion, other gowns like the rose silk gown and the blue, to hang in her wardrobe.

So intent was she on her thoughts that Miss Tibbles did not even notice the commotion her appearance caused in the taproom on the other side of the leaded glass windows of the posting house. Even she, however, could not ignore the six gentlemen who presently surrounded her.

Every one of the husbands of the Earl of Westcott's daughters. And Colonel Merriweather.

Marian felt a mixture of both chagrin and fond gratitude. That these men were here was a sign of the concern and affection the Westcott girls had for her and she could not but be gratified. On the other hand, she was Miss Tibbles and every one of them ought to have known that she was perfectly capable of looking after herself.

There was also the question of what Andrew was doing in the midst of these men! And that was the first question she blurted out.

"These men," Colonel Merriweather said, with patent irritation, "insisted upon watching for your return. As I did. We therefore found ourselves, perforce, in each other's company."

"There was more to it than that," Rowland added grimly. "We were concerned about you, Miss Tibbles. We wished to make certain nothing had, nothing would, happen to you. That Colonel Merriweather would treat you as he ought. Indeed, we believe he has some things to say to you."

Marian closed her eyes, hoping the lot of them would go away. She opened her eyes. They hadn't. They were all still there, bristling like bantam fighting cocks. She was neither amused nor pleased nor able to hold her tongue.

"How dare you?" she demanded, advancing on the lot of them. "How dare you presume to interfere in my plans this way? How did you know I did not wish to slip in and out of Bath unseen? How dare you presume that you are the proper judges of what is best for me?"

Marian could feel rather than see Merriweather's grin. He rocked back on his heels, thrust his hands behind him, and said to the others, "Told you. Told you that you weren't needed here."

The arrogance of all men! Now Marian rounded on the colonel. "And you!" she said, in the same minatory voice as before. "How dare you not tell me about my inheritance? How dare you presume to keep such a secret?"

One of the others started to speak and she quelled him with a single glance. Andrew held up his hands in defense. "I meant well," he protested.

He meant well! Marian advanced, slowly, giving Andrew the chance to retreat until his back was against the posting house wall. She stopped only when her toes touched his and, pulling herself to her full diminutive height, she glared at him, her face as close to his as possible.

"You meant well," she echoed sardonically. "How nice. But did it never occur to you that meaning well was not enough? That meaning well might do more harm than good? Or were you like the rest of your paltry sex, believing that whatever you decided must be better than anything I might choose to think or do myself?"

"I should never think that about you," someone said from behind her.

Marian turned, her eyes still flashing with anger. Then, because she didn't know which one had spoken, she addressed all five.

"Do not make bigger cakes of yourselves than you have already done!" she snapped. "The very fact that you are all here argues that you are just so foolish."

Then she rounded again on Andrew, who still stood pressed against the posting house wall. He had, she noted grimly, a stunned look upon his face. And he should!

"Well?" she demanded. "If this is an example of your thinking and the sort of tripe you meant to foist upon me after we were married, then I thank heavens I realized it in time! Or perhaps you ought to thank heaven, for I tell you clearly, Colonel Merriweather, that if you had found yourself leg-shackled to me, I should have told you precisely what I thought of such nonsense!"

"Cant terms, Miss Tibbles?" one of the others could not resist taunting her.

Marian turned. Slowly. She was, she decided, done with ringing a peal over Andrew's head. Now it was their turn again. So she advanced on them. They were either foolhardy or courageous for they did not scatter, as they might easily have done.

"You. Will. All. Go. Back. Home. Now. And tell your wives that I will not brook any further interference in my personal affairs! Is that understood?"

"Yes, Miss Tibbles," a meek chorus of five replied.

"Good," she said. Then, firmly grasping the one bag she had taken with her in her hand, she set off down the street in the direction of her lodgings.

The six men watched Miss Tibbles go, none daring or even wishing to attempt to follow her. Then the five brothers-in-law turned slowly to face Merriweather.

"The gentlest of women?" Berenford asked sardonically.

"You cannot imagine her ringing a peal over anyone's head?" Farrington chimed in.

"Completely unable to imagine her taking a pet?" Talbot threw in for good measure.

"Now, perhaps, you understand what we meant?" Winsborough asked.

"I do believe, gentlemen," Rowland said, watching Andrew carefully, "that he does."

Finally the colonel found his voice. "Good God! Is she often like this?"

"Only when she is crossed," Berenford assured him cordially.

"Only when she thinks you've been foolish," Talbot added his mite.

"Only—" Farrington began.

"All right!" Merriweather cut him short. "I understand. You need not say anything more."

"Have you never seen her like that before?" Rowland asked.

Had he? To be sure, she had been angry with him before. And even snapped at him a time or two. But somehow none of that had prepared him for her fury today.

Because it infuriated him that he had not anticipated such a thing, Andrew turned to Rowland and snapped, "If I had, do you think I would have been idiotish enough to spout the nonsense I did the other day?"

"Do you mean to cry off?" Farrington asked.

The others waited for his reply. Colonel Merriweather hesitated a moment, but then shook his head, a wry, sweet smile upon his face. "No. God help me, but despite everything, I do still love the woman."

Winsborough clapped a sympathetic hand on the colonel's shoulder. "Good luck, then. And let me assure you that while it is daunting, the first time you see Miss Tibbles in such a rage," he told him, "I assure you that she can be equally fervent in one's defense. I should back her against a whole army of villains, any day."

Andrew jutted out his jaw. "And I suppose the rest of

you consider me to be one of them?" he asked the others sarcastically.

"Oddly enough, no," Rowland said slowly. "I'll allow I did so, when I first came to Bath. But after the past couple of days in your company, Merriweather, I have come to believe I misjudged you. Mind, I wish I knew the answer to your odd behavior over this inheritance. And the truth about your first wife's death. But I do believe you genuinely care for Miss Tibbles."

"And even if he doesn't," Farrington drawled, "we've just seen that she would have no trouble and no hesitation in simply bowling him over."

There was some laughter, but it was more good-natured than Andrew might have expected. As the other men moved away and he turned in the direction of his own hotel, he thought that had he been in their shoes, he might not have been nearly so understanding.

He knew, none better, how odd his behavior must look. But he meant what he had said a few days before. He would tell Marian what was behind what he had done. But he would confide in no one else.

Andrew was congratulating himself on matters not having gone worse, and considering how to best approach Marian again, when he received the shock of his life. One that was almost more astounding than having his sweet Marian turn into a termagant such a short time before.

He was greeted at the door of his chambers by his batman, who said, in a voice that implied impending doom, "I have news, Colonel."

"Well? Spit it out!" Andrew said impatiently.

"It is your mother, sir. She is here in Bath."

Suddenly the colonel understood his batman's pallor. Abruptly he sank into the nearest chair.

"Here? In Bath?" he echoed in a hollow voice.

The batman nodded.

"Where? Where is she staying?" Andrew asked, trying to collect his thoughts.

"In this very hotel," the batman replied. "I encountered her maid, who informed me that they had arrived a few hours ago."

Andrew covered his eyes with his hand. "Why is my mother here? And I pray you won't tell me it is because of Miss Tibbles."

Despite his words, the colonel was not in the least surprised when his batman merely nodded. Andrew shuddered and rose to his feet.

"Very well. I suppose I had better go and see her."

"There is more," the batman said before he could move toward the door.

"More?"

"Your brother is here as well. Lord Merriweather has, I understand," the batman said, keeping his eyes very carefully fixed upon the ceiling, "brought the funds to buy the, er, 'brazen hussy off.' I believe, Colonel, those were the words his valet used."

Andrew closed his eyes then opened them again. He began moving again toward the door. "I've got to see him. Them. Both of them. And stop this nonsense before it gets any worse," he muttered to himself.

His batman's words stopped him once again.

"They are not here," he said.

Andrew glanced at the man, lifting his eyebrow in patent inquiry. The batman met his gaze now and scarcely flinched, though his voice was full of doom as he said, "They have gone to call upon Miss Tibbles."

Now Andrew waited no longer. He opened the door and took the steps down two at a time. He had to reach her lodgings and stand beside her. He had to show his mother and his brother that he truly did mean to marry Miss Tibbles and that they had best treat her with respect. If she would have him. After their encounter in the posting house yard he was no longer certain of any such thing.

But whether she would or not, he could not leave Marian to face his relatives alone. Not when it was a circumstance that even he would have found daunting in her shoes.

Chapter 23

Marian was very tired as she came in sight of her lodgings. She dearly hoped Mrs. Stonewell did not mean to be difficult, for she had no energy left for any further trouble today.

She stepped inside and was grateful to see that Mrs. Stonewell was nowhere in sight. Unfortunately, even as Marian put her foot on the first stair, the woman suddenly appeared. Her face was a study in malicious satisfaction as she told her, "You have visitors, Miss Tibbles."

"Who is it now?" she muttered to herself wearily.

"A Lord Merriweather and a Mrs. Merriweather," the landlady said with an air of triumph.

Marian blinked. That made no sense and she was far too tired to even try to comprehend what it meant. "I must go upstairs and change my gown," she said. "But then I shall be straight down."

Mrs. Stonewell made no objection but merely stood there watching as Marian mounted the stairs. Then she headed in the direction of the parlor, no doubt to inform Lord Merriweather and Mrs. Merriweather that Miss Tibbles would soon be down to see them.

By the time she had changed, as swiftly as she could because the names her landlady had given her told Marian these visitors must be relatives of Andrew's, she was in a rage again and in no mood for any more interfering fools.

Of course, she reminded herself as she came downstairs, no trace of her anger showing on her face, she might be mistaken. Lord Merriweather and Mrs. Merriweather might approve. They might be the first two people who did not attempt to interfere between herself and Andrew. But that, given her recent experiences, seemed most unlikely.

The moment Miss Tibbles opened the parlor door, she knew she was right. They were not here, this Lord Merriweather and Mrs. Merriweather, to congratulate her on her attachment to the colonel. Two pairs of eyes, hostility patent in them, turned immediately in her direction.

The gentleman, who bore a marked resemblance to Andrew, rose slowly, almost insolently to his feet. The woman, much older and perhaps his mother, remained seated and eyed Marian with a sour expression.

"Miss Tibbles?" the gentleman hazarded.

"Yes, of course this is Miss Tibbles," Mrs. Stonewell babbled. "No doubt you will wish to speak to her in private so I shall just be going."

No one said a word to stop her and Marian held the door open until the landlady had passed through. Then she quietly but firmly closed it. She came forward into the room and spoke, in a tranquil voice that belied the turmoil she felt inside.

"We will no doubt wish to keep our voices low for I suspect that Mrs. Stonewell is, as usual, listening at the door."

The other two looked taken aback and then the gentleman said, jutting out his jaw in a way so like Andrew had done, such a short time before, "We do not care what she may overhear."

"No, but perhaps I do," Marian said gently, gliding toward them. "You must recollect that, for the moment, I am living here."

"Impertinence!" the woman snapped.

Marian came to a halt midway between the two. In the same gentle voice as before she said, "I collect you are Mrs. Merriweather and Lord Merriweather and I presume you are related to Colonel Merriweather."

"He is my brother."

"My son."

Marian nodded. "Then you both no doubt have a great regard for him."

"We do," Lord Merriweather agreed, unbending just a trifle.

"Pray be seated," Miss Tibbles said, waving him to a seat as she took one herself.

There was a silence and Marian took a deep breath before she shattered it. "You have come, no doubt, because you have heard of your son's attachment to me and you wish to see just how shocking a mésalliance it might be?"

"Impudence!" Mrs. Merriweather snapped.

Marian shook her head. "No, I am merely speaking the truth. I have been a governess for eighteen years and I know that although my birth was perfectly respectable, that circumstance alone must seem to render me ineligible in the eyes of many. That plus my age."

"How much," Lord Merriweather demanded, his eyes once more hard and unfriendly.

Marian blinked. "I beg your pardon?"

"How much? How much do you want to shear off and never see my brother again?"

Miss Tibbles had come into the room intending, despite any possible provocation, to be polite to her visitors. She had vowed to herself that she would not allow any slights to pierce her skin. She was finding that her vows had been overly ambitious and she was not going to be able to keep them. Still, she tried.

"I am afraid you will find you cannot buy me off," Marian said calmly.

"I told you," Mrs. Merriweather said impatiently.

"You've got to make her an offer. A large one. And a promise to help her find a new post. Though we must make certain it is one where there are no impressionable males around," she added caustically.

Marian almost laughed, except that it hurt to know Andrew's family thought so ill of her and would go as far to detach him from her.

Again she said, "I can neither be bought nor frightened off. I do not need your funds nor another post. I have just come from London where I have learned that I have inherited an ample competence for my needs."

"Then you don't need to marry Andrew?" Mrs. Merriweather asked hopefully. "It was all a hum?"

"Told you it was a hum," Lord Merriweather said with some disgust. "Told you he wouldn't have fallen for a woman so far past her last prayers."

Her wretched temper would always be the failing of her, Marian thought, even as she felt herself rise to her feet. Even as she heard herself open her mouth and begin to speak she knew she shouldn't. But she did. If only he hadn't made that comment about her age!

Slowly, but with such strength of manner that neither of her visitors could possibly doubt that she meant what she said, Marian told them, "Oh, but you are mistaken. Andrew is attached to me. Deeply attached to me. And I to him. I think you will shortly discover that despite anything you might say, despite anything anyone might say, Andrew and I are going to be married. And there is not a blessed thing either of you can do to stop us."

Both Lord Merriweather and Mrs. Merriweather began to speak at the very same moment. They protested. They argued. They hurled curses and insults at her head. Marian stood unmoved by any of it. When their tempo slowed, when they seemed to be running short of words, only then did she deign to speak.

"You are being ridiculous," she said, shaking her head.

"All you can accomplish with this sort of behavior is to drive a wedge, irrevocably, between yourselves and Andrew. I am telling you this for your own good. If you ask him to choose between yourselves and me, I can tell you now that you will lose."

Then, all but shaking with rage, Marian calmly started toward the door of the parlor. Only the manner in which she wrenched it open betrayed the depth of emotion she felt. But, wrench it she did and promptly came face-to-face with Andrew, who stood right outside the parlor door, a foolish expression pasted on his face.

Marian faltered at the sight of him. She blushed as she recalled the last words she had said to him and compared them with the ones he might just now have overheard. With a sinking sensation, she realized that the smile on his face meant he almost certainly had heard.

Gently, soothingly, he turned her around and pushed her back into the parlor, firmly closing the door behind him. Once inside, he did not let her go but instead slid an arm around Marian's waist. It was a gesture she knew she should reprove him for. It was a gesture certain to inflame his brother and mother's already agitated nerves. And he very well seemed to know it.

"Mother. James," he said, acknowledging his kin. "What are you doing here? Come to welcome my betrothed to the family?"

His mother was the first to recover. "Don't be absurd!" she told him tartly. "You cannot marry this, this governess. What will people say?"

Colonel Merriweather told her precisely and quite pithily his complete indifference to the thought of what people might say about it.

"She is after your money," his brother warned.

Andrew smiled down at Marian in a way that made her feel far too warm and want to lean against him. But she quite properly did not, of course. Instead she waited for his answer.

"Don't you know?" he told his brother. "I am marrying another heiress."

"Don't even jest about such things!" his mother said impatiently.

Lord Merriweather was dismissive. "Yes, yes, she told us she has come into a small competence. But it can mean nothing to you. It cannot possibly make any sort of difference to your financial condition."

"No?" Andrew looked down again at Marian with a foolish smile still on his face. "Perhaps you are right. But I am far more concerned with the state of my heart than with the state of my finances."

"Preposterous!" Lord Merriweather sputtered.

"I will not stand for this!" Mrs. Merriweather said coldly.

Andrew moved his hand from Marian's waist to place it around her shoulders and draw her even closer. "No?" he said to his mother over the top of Marian's head. "A pity. Well, you may leave then. You as well, James. Marian and I have a wedding to plan."

Sputtering and arguing made no impression on Andrew. Within minutes he had somehow shepherded them out of the parlor so that he and Marian were alone.

"Did you mean it?" he asked. "Or did you tell my mother and brother you meant to marry me only because they roused your temper?"

Miss Tibbles had the grace to blush. Still, she tilted her nose into the air and sniffed as she said, "You are a fine one to talk! I've no doubt you did the very same thing. After all," she said, losing her haughty air, "you cannot possibly still wish to marry me, now that you know what a termagant I can be."

He kissed the tip of her nose. "Yes, but such a delightful termagant."

He said it lightly, playfully, and Marian found herself very much wanting to believe him. Her forehead wrinkled as she looked up at him.

"Do you truly mean it?" she asked. "That you wish to marry me? I cannot think why."

"Because of your fortune, of course," he said promptly, mischief dancing in his eyes.

She shook her head. "We both know that cannot be the case. Andrew, I wish you will tell me the truth. About how you found out about my inheritance. About why you went to the solicitor. And why you didn't tell me of it. And about what happened to your first wife."

She held her breath, half afraid he would either round on her or stalk off in anger. She could read in his face that he was strongly tempted to do either or both.

Instead he shrugged and said, ruefully, "If there is ever a chance for us to be happily wed I've no choice but to do so, have I?"

"None," she agreed softly.

He nodded, his eyes fixed on a spot on the wall, and Marian knew his thoughts must be very far away. She waited patiently, knowing this could not be an easy step for him to take.

She didn't know what the answers were but she knew, now, deep in her heart, that they were, that they could only be, honorable ones.

So she waited. And in the end, he said, quietly, "I'll return this evening and answer your questions then. If you will be patient that long?"

Marian nodded. "Until this evening. But," she added, reverting to her stern self, "no longer. You are going to tell me the truth!"

In answer, he only grinned fondly and kissed the tip of her nose again. It was, she thought, becoming quite a habit with him and she could not quite decide whether she liked it or ought to reprove him for it, just on principle. In the end, before she could make up her mind, he was moving toward the door.

"My dearest Marian," he said lightly, teasingly, "I shouldn't dream of risking the rise of your temper ever again. Certainly not so soon after this afternoon. Why, you had me positively quaking in my boots!"

She snorted but could not find it in her heart to reprove him. Indeed, she was all but certain there was the most absurd, fond, smile upon her face.

There was and it was enough to warm both of them for the next several hours.

Until evening, when he would finally tell her the truth.

Chapter 24

Colonel Merriweather found his rooms at the White Hart invaded by both his brother and his mother. Fortunately his batman had hovered around, downstairs, so as to be able to warn him.

"A rare taking they look to be in, Colonel," the man told Andrew.

He smiled wryly. "That was to have been expected. Had my wits not gone begging I should have arranged for you to transfer us to another hotel the moment I knew they were in Bath! Well, it cannot be helped. I suppose I had best go up and see them."

"You could go out. Take your dinner somewheres else," the batman offered.

Andrew was undeniably tempted. And for a moment he seriously considered doing so. Even his mother and brother would not have the doggedness to still be waiting if he came back five hours later.

But then he shook his head. That would only postpone the inevitable and make them angrier than they already were. So instead he clapped his batman on the shoulder, thanked him for the warning, and headed upstairs for the confrontation he knew could not be avoided.

Andrew was not in the least surprised to find his brother pacing about the room and his mother engaged in looking over his clothes and loudly proclaiming that they all ought to be replaced with ones that were finer.

Another man would definitely have quailed at facing them. Andrew quietly entered the room and watched them for some moments before he spoke. Finally he said, "Well, how cozy. And is there nothing to be found here that meets the approval of either one of you?"

James started and muttered an imprecation. Then he held up his glass and told Andrew, "You've a fine brandy, at any rate."

His mother glared at both of her sons. She came toward Andrew and tried to conceal her anger and speak soothingly. She failed signally.

"There you are, dearest. Wherever have you been, we have been worried about you."

"I have been walking," he said curtly.

That drew a raised eyebrow from his brother. His mother, however, merely nodded and said, "Of course. This has been a trying day for you. Very trying. We understand completely, James and I."

"Do you?" Andrew raised a skeptical eye. "Then I wish you will explain it to me."

His mother pretended to laugh. "You are jesting, of course. I know better than to take the things you say entirely seriously. Including what you said when we saw that dreadful woman, Miss Tibbles."

Andrew gritted his teeth and waited. He was curious to see what strategy his mother would attempt next. When he did not answer her, she looked at him sharply, but undaunted, she plunged on.

"I would not wish to interfere in any of my children's lives, but I should be remiss if I did not warn you about women like Miss Tibbles. Surely, dearest, now that you are out of her company, you can see how absurd such a connection would be."

"I do not."

Now his brother spoke. "Dash it all, Andrew! You must. Not that I mean to say anything against the woman, and if you meant to set her up, well, er, never mind that," he added hastily as his mother glared at him. "Perhaps not. But you certainly cannot marry her. Why we've half promised you to Lord Peckwith's daughter."

Andrew let his eyes narrow. He did not trouble to hide the anger in his voice as he said, "Peckwith's daughter? The one with the squint and the horrid temper? The one who is scarcely two years out of the schoolroom?"

Lord Merriweather quailed before his brother's anger but Lady Merriweather was made of more stubborn stuff.

"Nonsense!" she said sharply. "Of course she will wear spectacles at home and then she will have no need to squint. As for her temper, if you lived in Peckwith's household, your temper would be uneven, too."

There was, Andrew had to acknowledge, some truth to that. Still, his mother spoiled it by going on. "As for her being scarcely out of the schoolroom, why, all the better. You will be able to mold her into just the sort of wife you wish. I doubt very much you will be able to mold Miss Tibbles at all. She is absurdly opinionated for a woman!"

Andrew considered, for a moment, the image of his bride-to-be and he smiled. "No," he conceded, "I do not think one could mold her at all."

His mother nodded with satisfaction. "There. You see? It makes far more sense for you to marry the Peckwith girl, now doesn't it?"

"Why?"

"Why?" His mother's equanimity faltered as she echoed his question. She became fluttery and avoided meeting his eyes as she tried to find an answer.

"Cut line, Mama, and tell me the truth!" Andrew said curtly.

Now she did look at him. Mrs. Merriweather shrugged and said, petulantly, "Oh, very well. You know that Peckwith's land marches with James's. We never expected that he would inherit it for I was certain your uncle would have a son. But Cordelia kept throwing out girls and then he died so suddenly. Well, it was too late for James. He was already married. And a quite sensible match it was, too, considering that we did not know he would inherit your uncle's land and title. But now it is in our part of the family and we must all look for ways to increase it. And you could do your part by marrying the Peckwith girl. It really isn't such a great sacrifice to ask you to make, after all."

Andrew had always known that his mother was selfish. He had even known that she passed on her curious way of looking at the world to his brother. But from having been out of the country, serving on the Continent for so long, he had almost forgotten just how curious it could be.

Once he had been sympathetic to her and fallen in with her odd plans. Now all he had to do was conjure up the image of Marian's face and he had no difficulty whatsoever resisting his mother's blandishments.

"No," he said curtly.

"No?" James echoed.

Their eyes met steadily and for once Andrew felt as though his brother truly understood. James was the first to give way. He sighed, took another deep drink of his brandy, then set the glass down with a snap.

"Come along, Mama. It is useless to argue with Andrew any longer. You and I had best accustom ourselves to the notion that Miss Tibbles is about to enter the family and try to make the best of it."

Mrs. Merriweather gasped in outrage but Andrew took a step toward his brother and they clasped hands. "Thank you," he said softly.

James's eyes were rueful as he said, "I still think you are making a mistake, but it is your mistake to make. In your shoes I would probably do so also. Good luck and may you find happiness with your little governess."

In spite of himself, Andrew grinned. "I shall," he promised.

Mrs. Merriweather looked from one of them to the other. "No," she said indignantly. "I cannot believe you will tolerate this, James. You are the head of the family, now. Do something!"

"I am," he said, heading for the door. "I am going to go and bespeak the finest dinner this damnable inn has to offer. Then I am going to drink several glasses of brandy. And finally, when I can drink no more, I am going to find my bed and go to sleep. I strongly advise you to do the same, Mother."

She sputtered some more but there really was nothing she could do. Andrew watched them leave his rooms with a strong sense of relief.

Then, before his batman could return, he moved quickly to the hiding place where he kept Drusilla's journal. Tonight he would give it to Marian. God help him if his judgment was wrong and she did not understand!

Colonel Merriweather was true to his word. It was dusk when he returned to Miss Tibbles' lodgings. He half thought the landlady would tell him the hour was too late and try to bar his way, but a generous coin, slipped into Mrs. Stonewell's discreetly outstretched hand, went a long way toward softening her resolve.

When Marian came into the room, Andrew found himself thinking she looked more beautiful than ever. He knew that was a word very few people would ever use for her. But she was beautiful. In her heart, where it truly mattered.

And when she looked at him with just that degree of warmth and, he was certain, longing, it was enough to almost unman him. So now he cleared his throat and said, "Thank you for seeing me, Marian."

She tilted her head to one side and smiled mischievously. "How could I not?" she teased him. "When you had promised at last to solve the mysteries that have been plaguing me for so long."

When he stood there, just gazing at her, Marian's expression altered, just a trifle. "Perhaps we should be seated?" she suggested, her eyes narrowing.

Recollecting the events at the posting house, Andrew made haste to agree. He did not, he realized, wish to rouse her temper twice in one day. And he was a reasonable enough man to understand that his behavior must seem maddeningly confusing to one who did not know what was behind it.

So he waited until Miss Tibbles had taken a seat, then Andrew placed himself by her side. He drew out from beneath his coat a parcel wrapped in sharkskin. At her quizzical look he shrugged.

"I have carried it with me through rain and mud. I needed to be certain nothing would damage it."

Marian took the parcel and slowly began to unwrap it. More than words could have done, the lack of haste with which she did so told Andrew that she already trusted him, without yet having heard an explanation, without yet knowing what he was giving her.

He felt an odd lightness in his heart and knew himself to be the most fortunate man in creation.

"It is a book," Marian said, confusion evident in her voice.

"A journal," he corrected her. "A journal of my first wife's thoughts. I have never shown it to anyone else. You must promise me that you will never tell anyone what is in these pages."

She looked at him for a long moment. It was not, he thought, in her nature to be so secretive. No doubt her many years as a governess, to girls who asked just such promises of her, had taught her to be wary.

Finally she said, slowly, "I promise, Andrew, that I

shall never tell anyone what is in these pages unless I have your permission to do so."

How like her to think of such a caveat! He smiled and gave a sigh of relief. Then he placed his hand over hers. "I beg you will take this journal and read it. After you are done, send for me and I will then answer all your questions. Questions that cannot be answered until you understand what is written here."

She continued to look at him quizzically, but there was no impatience or anger in her gaze, only sympathy. As though instinctively she understood how difficult it had been for him to take this step.

He rose to his feet before he could change his mind and snatch the journal back from her. For that was what he wanted very much to do. But he could not. Not if they were to be married for he would not wed Marian with such a heavy secret between them.

She did not protest his leaving her side. Instead she clutched the journal close to her breast and said, "I will take very good care of this." She paused and then added, "You need not be afraid I shall judge you harshly for anything she might say."

He touched her cheek and smiled, but there was far too much pain in that smile. "Make no promises now. You have not read it yet."

Then, before either of them could say anything more, Colonel Merriweather turned and swiftly left the room. Behind him he could hear Miss Tibbles gather up the sharkskin and wrap it around the book again.

In the hallway he met the landlady and, with a suppressed sigh, pressed still another coin into her hand. Then it was outside and into the chill night air.

Andrew began to walk.

Miss Tibbles slipped past Mrs. Stonewell, and up the stairs to her room, while the landlady was occupied showing Colonel Merriweather to the door. There Marian carefully locked her door and lit some candles so that she could read the journal Andrew had given her.

For a long moment she just sat in the chair, with the journal on her lap, before she opened it. His first wife's thoughts, Andrew had said.

It was almost frightening to think how important this was to him. To know that it had been written by a woman who had died so young and carried secrets so dark that Andrew could not bear to share them with anyone but herself.

But Miss Tibbles had never allowed herself to give way to such nonsense before and it was not very long before she took a deep breath, opened the journal, and began to read. It was, however, a very long time, indeed, before she set it down again. And when she did, it was knowing that it would be hard to wait until morning to read the rest.

Already Marian had a good sense of what Andrew's first marriage must have been like. And why he would have found it so hard to share this journal with anyone. Why he would have kept it so close to his heart. If only he had been able to share it with her from the start. But she could understand why that had not been possible.

Chapter 25

Miss Tibbles sent a note around to Colonel Merri-weather, asking him to call upon her, two days later. It took her that long to read the journal all the way through, for it was not an easy thing to read. And there was more than one place she needed to read twice or even three times.

She was waiting in the parlor when he arrived, but she wore her spencer and bonnet, a clear sign Marian knew he would want to go outside to talk. A clear sign she understood he would want to know they could not be overheard.

Andrew smiled at her and she felt her heart turn over. She was too old, she tried to tell herself, to feel this way. But she did. Just as she ought to be too old to feel such warmth run through her when he took her hand in his. But she did. And she certainly ought to be past the age of wanting, impulsively, to kiss him. But oh, despite everything, how very, very much she did!

It was hard to be patient as they walked to the stables where Merriweather had arranged for a carriage. It was already provisioned with a blanket and a basket of food. Marian blushed as she recalled the last time they had gone for a picnic but she did not draw back when it was time to be handed into the carriage.

She merely said, "You were confident."

He smiled wryly. "Let us say rather that I preferred to

be prepared, in the event I was fortunate enough to have you agree to come out with me. If you had not, well"— he paused and shrugged—"I should have been preoccupied with far more than the cost of a basket of food and the hire of a horse and carriage for the day."

Marian did not know how to answer this and she did not try. Instead she allowed him to hand her into the carriage without saying a word.

Andrew seemed to share her mood for he did not speak, either, until they were well clear of the town. Fortunately the day was a fine one and there was only a hint in the air of the colder weather soon to come.

He drove to the same picnic spot as before. And he went through the same ritual of preparing the blanket and basket. But this time he made no move to unpack the food. Instead he handed her to a seat with her back to a nice, large rock and sat himself facing her.

"You read Drusilla's journal?"

Marian nodded. "It must have been hard for you," she said.

He looked away and started to speak, then stopped himself. She could see the effort it took for him to meet her eyes again, but he did so.

"It was very hard," he agreed. "I loved her. Desperately. And at first, I thought her moods the result of a youthful nature. I thought her wild laughter a charming thing."

He stopped and took a breath. For a moment his eyes seemed to focus very far away. But then he looked back at her and made himself go on.

"For years I was away and when I could get home to see Drusilla, she seemed normal, albeit a little eccentric. But I put that down to the strain of being married to a man she rarely saw. I blamed myself for having married her at all while I still held my commission. But she urged me not to sell out. She assured me—frequently—that she didn't mind living with her family until I should be free to be with her all of the time."

Again he paused. Again he swallowed hard. There was a thin line of pain through his voice when he finally went on. "Drusilla said there would be time enough to have a home of her own later. And I believed her. Indeed, I thought her much like Kitty Pakenham, who waited eight years to marry Wellington. I thought her as wonderfully loyal and devoted to me and to my best interests. I had no notion that she and her family hoped to conceal matters from me as long as possible. That she was afraid to be a wife."

There was such self-condemnation in Andrew's voice that Marian couldn't bear it. Despite her promise to herself to do nothing until he had finished telling his story, she reached out and put her hand over his. He smiled and forced himself to go on.

"Eventually the war was over. It was possible for a wife to join her husband and be quartered with him. There were no more excuses left. And I swear Drusilla wanted to come to Paris. At least, I thought she did. It was only when I had her with me every day that I began to notice little things. But even then, God help me, I did not know the full extent of her madness until after her body was found and I discovered her journal."

"Why didn't you tell anyone?" Marian asked. "When they suspected you of her murder? Why didn't you tell them she took her own life?"

"How could I?" Andrew asked, pleading with her to understand. "Drusilla was so unhappy in life and I could not bear to have anyone think ill of her after her death. And, oh, I suppose a part of me felt as though I was to blame. As if their accusations were true in spirit, if not in the actual fact. It is only now, when I have had time to recover from her death, and talk with her family, that I know nothing I could have done would have prevented it."

Marian nodded. "I knew it the moment I read her journal. Drusilla was evidently unhappy for a very long time and I do not think anyone could have made her feel otherwise. In her words, she reveals her knowledge of how easily she slipped in and out of madness, of hearing voices, of thinking horrid thoughts. Her death was not your fault. I am so very glad that you are able to see it, too."

She paused and took a deep breath. "But this is not enough, Andrew."

He looked at her, startled, and it was her turn to have to force herself to go on. "It is not enough to lay to rest the rumors about your wife's death. There are other things between us. How did you learn of my inheritance? And why did you never tell me?"

He laughed, but it was a bitter laugh. "Because I am a fool!" he said. But then his voice grew more sober. "After Drusilla died, and I talked with her family and those who knew her family well, I began to realize she was not the only one in her family to suffer from madness. I began to realize that there were warning signs, had I only known where to look. And so, when I met you here and began to realize how drawn I was to you, I resolved to hire a Bow Street Runner and find out all I could about you."

He looked at her, a wry smile on his face, a look in his eyes that again begged her to understand.

"I was determined to make certain that madness did not run in your family as well. Particularly after I learned your father had killed himself. It was the Runner who discovered your aunt had died and left you an inheritance. I went to speak to the solicitor myself, to make certain it was true, before I told you. And I did mean to tell you. But I wanted to marry you and I thought, fool that I am, that the finest wedding present I could give you would be to tell you about your inheritance on our wedding night. And to give you papers then that would forever place its control in your own hands and not mine."

"Oh, Andrew," Miss Tibbles said.

She felt as though tears were welling up in her eyes and, the next thing she knew, she was sitting on Andrew's lap, her head pressed against his chest as his hands gently stroked her back.

When he felt her distress ease, he said, teasingly, "Now may we be married, Miss Tibbles?"

Marian laughed, she could not help herself. But it was not that simple and she knew it. She drew back and looked up at him. Her own voice was serious as she spoke.

"Andrew, you must know I am almost certainly past the age of bearing children for you. Are you certain you will never regret not fathering any offspring?"

He shook his head vehemently. "Never. So long as I have you, I shall always be content."

"But your mother?" she persisted. "Will she not expect you to give her grandchildren?"

Andrew gave a sharp laugh. "She is more likely, my love, to be delighted to know that my estate, upon my death, will help to enlarge that of my brother James and his engaging brood."

That, she decided, giving in to her baser impulses, deserved a kiss. Several moments later it was Andrew who lifted his head and demanded sternly, "Now are we done with objections? Now may we be wed?"

Marian hesitated and bit her lower lip. Andrew sighed a very exaggerated sigh. "Very well. What is it now?" he asked.

"Will we deal together well?" she asked. "You and I are both accustomed to giving orders. And being obeyed. I do not think either one of us can change. Will that not cause trouble between us?"

"And if it does?" he countered fondly. "Would you not rather have a lifetime of happiness together, punctuated by occasional arguments between us, than spend the rest of your life alone?"

Marian pulled herself free and rose to her feet. Determinedly she set some distance between them and took a very deep breath before she spoke.

"It is not so simple, Andrew. I blame myself. I should never have let matters reach this point. I ought to have cried off long ago. And I meant to do so."

"But why?" he asked bewildered. "You feel about me as I do about you and you can give me no real objections that matter! I thought that with the issues of my wife's death and your inheritance resolved there were no further barriers between us."

Marian smiled at him but her expression was strained. "I know you must think me absurdly missish—" she began.

"Yes I do think you are being absurdly missish," he agreed as he grumbled and rose to his own feet.

He started to advance toward her and Marian held up a hand to forestall him. "Listen to me," she pleaded.

Andrew stopped where he was, his fists clenched at his side as he forced himself to stand still. "I am listening," he told her, "but there is nothing you can say that will change my mind."

"No?" she asked, her eyebrows arched. "Consider, Andrew! I have been a governess for eighteen years!"

"I don't care," he answered stubbornly.

"The world will," she told him softly.

He consigned the world to the devil.

"Don't you see?" Marian asked, a hint of desperation in her voice. "I have been a governess. A servant. My life has not been conducive to being the kind of woman you must want as a wife. You want someone who has been

learning to be a lady, not someone who has been learning
how to be in service."

"I want you," he retorted, his voice blunt.

She opened her mouth to object and this time it was he
who stopped her. Andrew took a step forward. She retreated. He took another. And then several more. Marian
found herself backed against a tree as he stood before her.

"I have listened to far too much nonsense from you!"
he said, with exasperation. "Do you think sleeping in rain
and mud and wiping blood from my eyes is conducive to
gentility? To being a gentleman? Do you truly think my
life has been any more conventional than yours?"

Marian flinched at his scathing tone. "No," was all she
dared answer.

"Damnably right it was not!" Andrew flung at her.
Then his voice gentled, softened, and warmed as he
smiled and reached out to take her hand.

"Don't you understand, Marian?" he asked coaxingly.
"I want, I need a wife like you. Someone who will not expect me to be a mindless gentleman who thinks of nothing more than the cut of his coat, the throw of a dice, or
the turn of a card. I cannot play the games that gentlemen
play, of paying pretty compliments and pretending all is
always right with the world. I have seen too much that
was otherwise.

"I want a wife exactly like you, Marian. A woman who
will understand that the world is a complicated place. A
woman who will speak freely with me, one who has a
strength to match my own. Can you truly tell me that you
do not? Can you honestly tell me you believe that a hot-
house flower would suit me better?"

Marian could only shake her head. And when he
opened his arms, she could only go into them. He held
her close and kissed her with a fervency which gratified
her heart. She returned his embrace with a fervency that
could only gratify his.

It was some time before either one of them recollected the food and only then because Marian's stomach began to grumble. They both laughed as they opened the basket. There they found that Andrew's batman had thoughtfully provided a bottle of champagne.

"Cheeky fellow!" Andrew snorted, trying to sound stern but not succeeding.

"Very kind fellow," Marian countered, reaching for a glass. "I am certain you ought to raise his salary."

Andrew snorted again. "Are you already telling me what to do? Already ordering me about?" he demanded.

"Yes," she said, quite placidly.

"Ah. I thought you were." He smiled fondly at her, then added, "I shall have to think of some suitable orders to give to you."

Marian raised an eyebrow. "You may certainly try," she agreed, a twinkle in her own eyes. "Though I warn you here and now I am not likely to follow them. Do you want to cry off, sir?"

"Never!" he said with mock bravado. "I know I shall be horribly henpecked and my friends will all roast me, but I shan't care. I shall bear my burden willingly. Command me as you will."

"Command you?" Marian echoed, then shook her head. She looked at him with suddenly serious eyes. "Do you know, Andrew, for all our jesting, I think we shall, neither of us, truly wish to give orders to the other. We shall, at least I hope we shall, rather wish to talk with one another and reach decisions together."

Andrew set down his food and held out his hand. Marian took it willingly, allowing him to draw her to his side.

"I can think of nothing I should like better," he said in a husky voice, "than to reach decisions together with you, my love. We shall be the most scandalous couple! Living forever in one another's pocket and sharing each triumph and each ill. And I can imagine nothing I should like more."

Marian sighed and leaned closer. "There is one little thing," she said fingering a button of his coat.

"What?" he asked wary of her tone.

She lifted her head and he could see the laughter in her eyes. "I think," she said with a solemnity belied by just that look, "that we ought to make a pact always to be affectionate with one another. To be generous with embraces and other gestures of affection."

"Do you mean like this?" he asked with equally mock solemnity.

And he kissed her. Quite, quite thoroughly. When, sometime later, Marian had regained her breath, she replied, "Why, yes, that is precisely what I had in mind!"

It was scandalously late when they returned to town.

Epilogue

Marian and Andrew stood surrounded by a very large crowd of people, all of them smiling. How very much had changed in the past year!

Mrs. Merriweather kissed Marian on the cheek as she said, "My dear, I am so delighted that you have given me such a beautiful granddaughter."

Lord Merriweather clapped Andrew on the shoulder. "Well, I thought you a fool at the time, but I must admit that you were quite right to marry her. You are very lucky and I hope you know it."

Gazing at his wife, Andrew smiled and said, "I do, James. And am grateful every day that I found her."

All around them children ran, chasing one another across the back lawn of Colonel Merriweather's estate. They were the collective offspring of Lord Merriweather and his wife and all of the Earl of Westcott's daughters.

The earl and countess and daughters and sons-in-law were present but making very little effort to rein in the wildness of the children. It was, after all, too beautiful a day, on too beautiful an estate, to bother doing so. And they were far too busy enjoying the sight of Marian in such a patently happy state.

The guest of honor, little Elizabeth Merriweather, lay sound asleep in her cradle, which had been carried out and set under a tree so that all the world could admire her.

Marian went to where Andrew stood watching everyone cooing over their daughter. At precisely the same moment, they looked at one another.

"My mother is right," Andrew said softly. "She is a beauty."

Marian nodded, not trusting herself to speak.

He looked cautiously around. "Do you think," he whispered to her, "that anyone will notice if we slip away, just for a little while?"

Marian smiled, a mischievous air about her, as she said, "I think that if we were to slip into the maze no one would be likely to soon find us. How fortunate and how clever that someone thought to put it there!"

Something crossed his face, some trace of sorrow and instantly Marian was contrite. "Do you still miss her?" she asked softly.

There was no need to ask who she meant. Andrew shook his head. "I shall always think of Drusilla when I am in certain parts of the estate, like the maze, but she was who she was and she is gone. We are here and I am not such a fool as to miss her when I have you. If I have any regrets, it is that I did not find you, all those years ago, to tell you about Freddy Carrington's death."

When Marian blushed, as he knew she would, he kissed her. And then, in perfect accord, knowing full well that little Elizabeth, their miracle child, would be well looked after, the two joined hands and slipped away and out of sight.

If Elizabeth was a miracle child then, so, too, was their marriage a miracle. A miracle they did not intend, either Andrew or Marian, ever to take for granted.